"Have yo one kind

Dot's question thing you've ever said to me that wasn't cutting, humiliating or belittling?"

"Yes. I once told you you had beautiful eyes. Is that the kind of thing you want me to say?"

"Of course not," she said in confusion. "I don't want empty compliments, Calum."

"But it wasn't an empty compliment," Calum replied softly. "Your eyes are truly remarkably beautiful. Sometimes they have the look of a virgin, or some gentle creature that hardly knows the world. At other times they flash, like gray fires. And that mouth."

He reached out to touch the satiny skin of her lower lip. "Cool, touch-me-not, slightly arrogant. Yet so soft, so enticing...."

Madeleine Ker is a self-described "compulsive writer." In fact, Madeleine has been known to deliver six romances in less than a year. She is married and lives in Spain.

Books by Madeleine Ker

PASSION'S
FAR SHORE

Madeleine Ker

Harlequin Books

TORONTO • NEW YORK • LONDON
AMSTERDAM • PARIS • SYDNEY • HAMBURG
STOCKHOLM • ATHENS • TOKYO • MILAN

Original hardcover edition published in 1989
by Mills & Boon Limited

ISBN 0-373-03063-0

Harlequin Romance first edition July 1990

CHAPTER ONE

'OH, SUSIE, you must be kidding!'

'I'm not. I think it's a fabulous opportunity.'

'But *Japan*? I don't know a thing about Japan except *sayonara*, *sake* and *samurais*.'

'Well, that's a start.'

'Not enough of a start. In fact,' said Dorothy, using her slim fingers to nibble the advertisement out of the newspaper, nevertheless, 'I've never had even the faintest desire to go to Japan.'

They were sitting in the midst of a busy fast-food bar, just off Oxford Street, near where Susie worked. 'Read it again,' Susie commanded.

Dorothy consulted the square she had torn out. 'It says, "English governess wanted for four-year-old girl, living in Japan. All expenses, live-in accommodation, excellent salary to right applicant." And there's a phone number. That's all.' Dorothy gnawed her lower lip. Hers was a warm, mobile mouth, its fullness hinting at a nature both generous and impetuous. '"Live-in accommodation",' she repeated thoughtfully. 'Do you think they're a Japanese family?'

'I doubt it. But there's only one way to find out.'

'I don't know...'

'Well, it's the best job in the smalls all week,' Susie said practically. 'All the others you've looked at have been duds. And there's obviously a whacking great salary. And you love travelling. You're the galloping governess.'

'But Japan's so far away. So remote. It's the other side of the world.'

'Exactly. When would you ever get to a country like Japan in the normal course of things?' Susie nodded at the advertisement. 'That promises all the things you love best—a challenge, excitement, adventure, foreign food.' Susie took another bite of her hamburger, and Dot looked fondly at her friend's face, its dark prettiness unmarred by the bulge in one cheek made by the mouthful.

'Wouldn't you miss me if I went off to Japan for ever and a day?'

'Oh, I'd miss you *awfully*.' The bulge vanished, to reappear in Susie's other cheek. Susie's big brown eyes were earnest. 'But it probably won't be for more than a year—it never is. Now's your chance, love. It won't come again. Whatever happens, you won't be gone for ever.'

'What if a *samurai* gets me?'

Susie snorted. 'You should be so lucky! If anything gets you, it'll more likely be the *sake*.'

'Either way,' sighed Dot, 'it's *sayonara*.'

'But it would be *sayonara* just the same if you got a job in North Yorkshire, or the Outer Hebrides,' Susie pointed out. She wiped her dainty fingers clean on a paper napkin. 'There's a phone booth in that corner,' she pointed out. 'What have you got to lose? I'll buy us coffee while you ring.'

Dot opened her mouth to poke some more fun at the idea, then closed it again. What *did* she have to lose?

It was her duty to explore any and every avenue of employment, wasn't it? She was twenty-five, newly un-employed, and relatively unencumbered with ties, either emotional or financial. If she ever had a chance to enjoy a challenge, adventure, and the flavour of a foreign life-style, it was now. In six months' time it would be too late.

It was a thousand-to-one chance that she would be offered this job, anyway. And even if, by some remote chance, she *were* to be offered it...well, she could always turn it down then, and set a course for North Yorkshire or the Outer Hebrides.

Dorothy Beech had large, clear grey eyes, fringed with thick black lashes. When she stared into the middle distance, as she did now, their thoughtfulness seemed to radiate an aura of cool concentration that counteracted the passion of that warm mouth.

What the hell!

Acting on an impulse that had suddenly stung her like a mosquito, Dorothy rose to her feet, showed Susie her crossed fingers, and made her way through the restaurant towards the telephone, the advertisement in one hand.

Susie was smiling as she watched her friend's progress towards the telephone cubicle. What she saw was a tall, slender woman with beautiful legs and a head of glossy black hair that fell down her nape in tight curves that weren't quite curls. The cream dress was slightly over-formal; but with that face, and that figure, Dorothy Beech was attracting male glances from all around the restaurant. Wearing something more suitable to her age, rather than to the Swiss diplomat's residence where Dorothy had been working for the past six months, she would have been a sensation.

The phone call didn't take long. By the time Susie had queued for two cups of coffee and was heading back to their table, Dorothy was putting down the receiver.

'Well?' asked Susie as they sat down again.

'They were very nice.'

'Who are "they"?' Susie asked.

Dot consulted the note she had made. 'Osborne, Burgess & Salters. Solicitors in the Strand.'

'Solicitors?'

'They represent the people in Japan.'

'So you've got an interview?' Susie said in excitement.

'Friday afternoon at four,' Dot nodded. 'They want references from the Swiss people and a previous employer.'

'And they're keen to see you?'

'So it seems,' she agreed. 'I've never been interviewed by a solicitor before. I suppose the people couldn't come back to England just to interview a governess.' She was experiencing an ever so slightly fluttery feeling in the pit of her stomach. The pleasant-sounding male voice at the other end of the line had been enthusiastic, especially when she had told him her age. She picked up her coffee-cup. A flicker of excitement shot through her. 'Oh, Susie, what should I be doing? Boning up on Japan?'

'That might be a start.'

'I'll go and see what I can find in the library,' Dot mused. 'I should have asked him whereabouts in Japan the job was.'

'And you'll have to find something suitable to wear for the interview. What about a nice kimono, and a couple of knitting-needles stuck in your hair?'

Dot smiled. Susie glanced at her watch, mewed in dismay, and gulped down the rest of her coffee. 'I have to rush, darling. I've got to finish a drawing for four-thirty, or my boss will have my head. Ring me tonight, and we'll talk.'

'OK. I'll get the bill.'

'I'm the one in gainful employment. But I'll accept on the strength of Japan. Thanks, Dot.' They kissed hastily, and Susie hurried out to the advertising agency where she worked. Dorothy finished her coffee at more pensive leisure, paid the bill, and left a few minutes later.

The tube station was ten minutes' walk away from the restaurant where they had met, and Dorothy strolled thoughtfully in that direction.

She had enjoyed her last job, though it had lasted only six months. The Swiss children had been beautifully behaved, and her job of teaching them the English language, and about English ways, had been nothing but a pleasure. She had grown really fond of them, and she'd been sincerely upset when Herr Burckhardt had been posted to South America. Saying goodbye to them all, she had experienced a sense of loss that was still with her.

An occupational hazard of the job, she reminded herself. Growing to love other people's children had disadvantages as well as pleasures. And the only remedy for that was to marry some appropriate male, have a brood of her own, and settle down to bring her well-honed skills to bear on her own progeny.

But she knew that wasn't an answer, not at this stage of her life. Dorothy Beech wasn't ready to settle down yet. She enjoyed her independence far too much. And her job had given her enough insight into the married relationships of too many couples for her to have many romantic illusions about the state of matrimony. To settle down to the life of bickering, boredom and banality that most people seemed to call wedlock was a prospect that did not enchant her in the slightest.

On the other hand, Dot loved children, and was at her happiest working with them. Which was where the pleasures of being a governess came to the fore; you got the joy of children without the chains of marriage.

In fact, she had often reflected that she got the best of her employers' children. She had the daytime pleasures of playing with them, helping their budding minds start to flower, and entering that magical world of childhood imagination. All too often, the weary parents came back from work just in time to bath toddlers who were ready for bed, and had to share the day's adventures at second hand, through the governess's report.

It was a great pity, she reflected, getting back to the present, that the family weren't on hand for her to meet. 'Live-in accommodation' sometimes meant sharing life very closely with a family, and it was easy to get on one another's nerves, especially in a situation where there was little other companionship of your own nationality.

Nevertheless, she was getting more and more excited about Friday's interview.

A travel agent's window caught her eye, and she stopped to stare in. There was an enchantingly pretty poster of Mount Fujiyama in one of the displays, showing the pastel delicacy of cherry-blossom against the white serenity of the snow-clad cone.

But there were other images in her mind's eye, of crowded cities, teeming with all the problems of a highly competitive and technologically advanced society.

Both must be aspects, she supposed, of a very complex country. The idea of going to Japan was intriguingly different. Well, a little research in the Borough Library would clarify her ideas of a place in the world she knew next to nothing about, and might possibly harden her decision as to whether she really wanted this job or not.

On Friday afternoon at five to four, Dot was sitting in an impressively large office in the Strand, looking at a collection of sporting prints on the opposite wall. She had expected to find herself part of a large contingent of prospective governesses, but the waiting-room was empty of other applicants. There were only two very busy secretary-receptionists behind the mahogany desk.

She was in a state of some nerves. Despite her lack of confidence in the allure of Japan—her researches had left her more puzzled than otherwise about the country— Dorothy Beech was a person who hated to fail a challenge, any sort of challenge. She was determined to make a good impression, and she had taken a lot of time over her preparation, both physical and mental. Was she too smart? The rose-pink dress wasn't exactly governessy, but it suited her colouring. Bag and shoes, anyway, were unimpeachably sober, and her black hair was newly cut and styled in a businesslike crop.

At four o'clock precisely, a silver-haired woman of around sixty-five or seventy came in from the street outside. She was slim and smart. The suit she wore was modern and obviously expensive, and she carried herself with a briskness that belied her years.

She gave Dot a very searching glance from keen brown eyes that obviously didn't need spectacles. The secretary greeted her respectfully, and sent her into the inner sanctum of the office.

Shortly afterwards, the summons came for Dot herself to go in.

When she came into the office, the elderly woman was sitting across the desk from a tall, middle-aged man, who rose to extend his hand.

'Michael Osborne,' he introduced himself, letting his glasses drop on a loop round his neck. 'And this is Miss Barbara Hescott, who is the legal guardian of the child.'

'Pearl is my youngest nephew's daughter,' the elderly woman said without preamble. She was subjecting Dot to an even more piercing scrutiny. Her handshake was dry and brisk. 'I'm her technical guardian while she's in England, and my nephew has appointed me to interview for the post of governess.'

'Then she isn't in Japan?' asked Dot.

'Not yet. She's going out to join her father in a short while,' Barbara Hescott said. 'But please sit down. We can come to all that later on.'

'If we could have some basic details,' Michael Osborne suggested, unscrewing his fountain-pen. 'You've brought your references and curriculum vitae?'

Dot passed them over. She had assembled a folder containing all the details about herself that they might possibly want. Miss Hescott took the folder, and, while she concentrated on it intently, Dot answered a series of dry questions from the solicitor about her age, experience, and qualifications.

She had thought the elderly lady wasn't listening to the interrogation, but she looked up sharply after a while.

'How did you lose your last job?' she asked.

Dot explained about the Swiss diplomat, but the V-shaped frown remained between the other woman's eyes.

'You're very highly qualified, Miss Beech. You even have a university degree. I find it hard to believe that you can be dedicated to a job which will scarcely make any demands on the education you've had.'

'Oh, I can, and I am,' Dot assured her. 'I'm at my best with young children. I love them, and I have a vocation to look after them. I've been a governess for the past four years. And though it's true I'm university-trained, I don't think I'm over-qualified. It just means that my general knowledge is broad enough to cope with the educational needs of most children that age.'

'You could have been a schoolteacher, rather than a governess.'

'I've always felt that the best teaching relationships are one-to-one, but unfortunately that's not possible in

a school, even in the best schools. The idea of under-
taking the education of one or two children has always
appealed to me far more.'

The solicitor looked at Miss Hescott, then cocked his
head at Dot. 'Your qualifications are certainly impressive,' he observed. 'You even have a diploma in first-
aid.'

'It's surprising how often a little first-aid comes in
handy when superintending a family of adventurous
children,' Dot smiled.

'There are governesses' posts all over England,'
Michael Osborne suggested. 'Going to Japan is a serious
step, Miss Beech.'

'I realise that,' nodded Dot. 'But I enjoy a challenge,
and I love going to foreign countries.'

'You see this post as holding high amusement po-
tential?' Miss Hescott asked drily. 'Travel, adventure,
and so forth?'

'The prospect of living in Japan is certainly a challenge,' she said carefully. 'But that's not my main reason
for applying.' She looked at the other woman candidly.
'In fact, Miss Hescott, so far it's only the prospect of
going to Japan that puts me off this job. I have to say
that I'm not fully committed to the idea. I'll have a
clearer attitude towards it when I know how long my
services will be required for.'

There was the glimmer of a smile on Barbara
Hescott's mouth for a moment. 'You needn't have too
many fears on the score of not liking Japan. It's a fascinating country,' she said. But she did not take up Dot's
hint for further information. 'What ties do you have
here?'

'None. Not at the moment.'

'Haven't you got any family?' the solicitor enquired,
raising his eyebrows.

Miss Hescott gave him a quick glance. 'Miss Beech was the sole survivor of an accident in which her parents died, Michael,' she said quietly, and passed him the folder.

The solicitor's eyes widened. 'I'm so sorry.'

'It was a long time ago,' Dot said easily.

She was aware of the woman's eyes watching her. There was a depth to Barbara Hescott, shades of irony and wisdom that made Dot feel very young. Miss Hescott was definitely in command here. Observing her more closely, Dot had noticed that the diamonds she wore were dazzlingly impressive. Like the beautiful French suit, they spoke of wealth and taste. But for all that, Dot was now at her ease with her, feeling an odd sort of affinity with her.

'Men?' Miss Hescott now asked succinctly.

'None,' Dot replied, equally briefly. She wasn't going to go into any details about her private life at this stage, and she met Barbara Hescott's eyes squarely, catching once again that inner hint of amusement.

It was not until she had been exhaustively vetted that Miss Hescott turned to the lawyer with an authoritative air.

'Since we now know so much about Miss Beech, Michael, I think it's time she knew a little about the post she's applying for.'

'Of course,' the lawyer agreed.

'And I think we might stretch to a little refreshment.'

In response to the hint, the solicitor murmured a message into his intercom, and a secretary came in a moment later with a decanter of sherry and some biscuits.

'Not too early for you, is it?' asked Miss Hescott.

'No, I'd like a sherry, please.' Dorothy sipped the extra-dry *fino*, concentrating on keeping her poise. Her heart was beating a little faster, though. Getting as far as sherry and biscuits was obviously a good sign!

Michael Osborne steepled his long fingers and contemplated the middle distance. 'The little girl in question—Pearl Hescott—was four this summer. Her parents were divorced three years ago, and her father took up work in Japan a year after the estrangement. He has returned periodically to the UK since then, but has seen very little of his daughter since the divorce. He's currently working in Tokyo, for one of the Japanese electronics giants. I should mention that he is one of the foremost designers of electronic circuits for the computer industry, and a very successful man.'

The solicitor sipped his sherry, then resumed. 'But the situation has now changed drastically, in that the child's mother died four weeks ago—a yachting accident in the South of France.'

'I'm very sorry to hear that,' said Dot, taken aback.

'Mr Hescott now wants the child to join him in Japan. Clearly, however, he is not equipped to care for a four-year-old daughter on his own. That's why this post has been advertised.' He poured more sherry for them all. 'Mr Hescott will be in Japan for at least a further nine months. His plans after that are fluid. He may choose to stay on in Japan, or move to other work elsewhere in the world. At the end of the nine-month period, the successful applicant might possibly be asked to keep the post. It will be left open-ended on both sides.'

He went on to discuss the salary involved, which was substantially higher than anything Dot had been paid in the past, high enough to leave her with enough, if she saved diligently, to halve her mortgage on her flat.

'As the advertisement indicates,' he concluded, 'the successful applicant will be expected to live in Mr Hescott's house, and to form part of the family unit.'

'I see.' Again, Dot was aware of Barbara Hescott's eyes on her.

'Mr Hescott is naturally eager for his daughter to join him without delay. Ideally, the child should fly out to meet him within two weeks from today. It would be far better for the child to travel accompanied by her future governess, if that were possible. If you were offered the post, would you be able to leave London so soon?'

'Mr Hescott didn't come back——' Dot was about to say, 'for the funeral', but changed her tack diplomatically. 'He isn't coming back to collect the child?'

'Unfortunately he has been unable to free himself from the obligations of his work.'

Dot felt a flicker of distaste for such callousness, but hid it well. 'I see.' She thought hard. A fortnight gave her hardly any time to organise her departure. Not that she had much of a wardrobe to assemble, but she would need to think it out, and certainly do some extra shopping for a nine-month stay abroad. And there was the flat...though she could always ask the estate agency to rent it out in her absence, as she had done on previous occasions.

She nodded reluctantly. 'Well...it could be done, I suppose.'

'There must be things,' Barbara Hescott said, watching Dot with those wise brown eyes, 'that you would like to ask us, Miss Beech.'

'Well, yes, there are one or two things. How has Pearl reacted to her mother's death?'

'Pearl has no idea of the truth. She understands only that her mummy has gone away for a long time,' said Miss Hescott, 'and that she must now go to stay with her father.'

'Yes, I see.' Dot waited for the other woman to go on.

'I should also tell you that Pearl is a rather special child. She has certainly inherited her father's intelligence, and she looks as though she's probably inherited her mother's beauty into the bargain. She can be adorable when she's good. But she's a sensitive and sometimes difficult little girl, who will require a fair bit of effort on the part of whoever takes her on. She's been spoiled a lot, and seems to have managed to get her way by throwing tantrums whenever she was crossed.'

'Oh,' said Dot, wincing inwardly.

'But on the other hand, she responds badly to heavy-handed discipline. She's been in the company of adults a great deal since the divorce. Her mother tended to involve her very much in her own rather pleasure-orientated life-style, and that has had a strong influence on Pearl. I'm sure you know how disruptive that kind of up-bringing can make a child.' Barbara Hescott glanced at Dorothy.

'She expects to be treated like a little grown-up? Joining in all conversations and meals, going to bed when she pleases, that sort of thing?'

A subtle change took place in the other woman's face. 'Then you do understand. Add to that a very lively mind, and a genuine thirst for knowledge about the world, and you have an idea of Pearl's character. You've said that you enjoy a challenge. Does that sound like the sort of challenge you would enjoy?'

'Well, I think it's one I could cope with,' Dot replied neutrally. 'I take it Mr Hescott hasn't remarried?'

'No.'

'Then the family unit you've mentioned would consist of Mr Hescott, his daughter—and me?'

It was Miss Hescott who broke the awkward little silence. 'The first thing I should emphasise is that Calum, my nephew, is an exceptional person. He's not an angel by any means, but he's not the sort of man to take advantage of a woman under his own roof.'

'I see,' Dot said without inflections.

There was an ironic glitter in the brown eyes which Dot could not fathom. 'Calum has quite a large acquaintance, both Japanese and Western. His social life is reasonably full. The house is also maintained by several servants, who live on the premises, so there's no question of your being isolated with him. Besides which,' Miss Hescott concluded, folding her hands in her lap, 'I myself will be staying at the house for at least two months this winter. Calum and Pearl are my closest surviving relatives,' she explained, 'and if the mountain will not come to Mahomet, Mahomet must go to the mountain.' There was more than a hint there, Dot thought, that Barbara Hescott disapproved of her nephew's absence at this time. 'I take it you would consider me an adequate chaperon for at least a part of your spell in Japan?'

'That certainly makes a difference,' Dot said evenly. Women in her position were all too vulnerable. She was no stranger to having a charge's father make a pass at her, and the last thing she wanted was to find herself playing Jane Eyre to some brooding Mr Rochester with a Japanese setting.

Beside that, it hadn't escaped her attention that Miss Hescott was now talking as though she were going to offer Dot the job.

'Do you find the conditions a problem?' the solicitor asked.

Dot told the truth. 'I do, yes. This isn't an ordinary situation.' She hesitated, wondering how to put this delicately. 'The death of a mother leaves a big vacuum in a child's life—I know that from my own experience.'

'As I do from mine,' Barbara Hescott said quietly.

'Well then, you'll also know how easy it is for a child to transfer all her love to a mother-surrogate, like a governess. Then, when the relationship has to end...' She looked from one to the other, reflecting that probably neither had ever had much to do with small children or governesses. 'It's a situation I try never to get involved in. The consequences can be very painful—for the child, principally, but also for the governess. Speaking frankly, I would probably not wish to renew any contract at the end of nine months, especially if Mr Hescott continues to live abroad. Little Pearl sounds as though she needs someone who can give her a much longer-term commitment than I can offer.'

The solicitor said nothing, and it was Miss Hescott who spoke, her voice gentling. 'But spare mothers don't grow on trees, do they? To be quite blunt with you, Miss Beech, Pearl needs all the love she can get, permanent or temporary.'

'I can give her nine months' worth. And then what?'

There was another pause after Dot had said those perhaps unwise words. Then, acting on a glance from Barbara Hescott, Michael Osborne made a noise in his throat, indicating that the interview was drawing to a close. 'Then I think we'll leave it here for the time being.'

The three of them rose.

'We'll take up the references you've given us. You can see that our time-scale is rather tight,' Michael Osborne went on, as they headed towards the door, 'and I think it's safe to say that you can expect to hear from us one way or another within the next two days.'

'Thank you for coming, Miss Beech.' Barbara Hescott's handshake was longer than when they had first met, and she was wearing a smile that reached her brown eyes, warming their sometimes cold depths. 'I've enjoyed meeting you. We'll be in touch very soon.'

After exchanges of goodbyes, Dot left, noticing that two other women were now sitting in the waiting-room. Both were hefty, in their fifties, very grim-looking, and had 'governess' written all over them.

Out in the autumn sunlight, some of the post-interview euphoria started to fade. Yes, she was sure she had made a good impression, and might be seriously considered for the post. But did she really want it? If this job didn't work out, it was a long, long way home from Tokyo.

Little Pearl Hescott sounded both rather pathetic and rather dreadful. Pearl needed a mother, but Dot was only a governess. And that was the way it had to be. She couldn't spend the rest of her life devoted to a child who was not her own, no matter how much she enjoyed her work. Sooner or later, surely, Mr Right would come along, and she would stop working to have a stab at the bickering, boredom and banality. Slightly cynical as she was, she loved children far too much to think of remaining a professional spinster.

Living alone with the child and the child's father, in a very alien foreign land, was daunting enough. More so was the prospect of having a motherless child twine her way round her own heart. What would happen when the hour for parting came? An excruciatingly painful wrench for both of them.

It wasn't what she wanted.

What she wanted was a cheerful, happy household somewhere not too far from London, Susie, and the rest of her friends. Children who weren't problematic, a family that was stable and loving, a set of relationships that were manageable and without darker shadows.

If wishes were horses, she smiled a touch wryly. She hadn't ever had *that* level of perfection in a job to date.

But the cogs of her mind were meshing into a decision. She wouldn't take the job, even if it were offered. She didn't want it, and that was all.

Goodbye, Fujiyama.

It occurred to her to get back in touch with them, and ask them to scratch her off their list at once, but that seemed far too presumptuous a move. After all, the chickens weren't even hatched yet!

She crossed the hurly-burly of the Strand, heading for Charing Cross tube station, and the next train home.

'Miss Beech? It's Barbara Hescott here.'

'Oh, hello, Miss Hescott.' Dot put the mixing-bowl down. She was in the kitchen of her flat, trying her hand at a cake. Her hands were all flour, and she moved the receiver to her other ear, trying to use her wrists.

'I hope I haven't caught you at an inconvenient moment?'

'Not at all,' Dot lied. Her heart was beating rather heavily. It was two days since the interview. If she was about to be offered the job, she would have to tell Miss Hescott she wasn't interested.

But she was to be surprised. 'I'm calling from my flat in Highgate. I have Pearl with me. I'd like you to come and have tea with us this afternoon.'

Dot took a breath. 'Miss Hescott, I've decided——'

'Nothing to do with the job,' Miss Hescott's voice cut in briskly. 'I'd just like you to meet the child. I feel I need a little professional advice about her, which you may be able to give me.'

'Oh.' Put like that, a refusal would be churlish. Drat it, the woman must have a sixth sense! She would have to postpone her refusal until they met.

Reluctantly, Dot nodded. 'Well, thank you very much. What time would you like me?'

'I'll send my chauffeur to pick you up at four, if that suits you.'

Chauffeur? Dot hesitated. 'It would be so much easier by Tube——'

'It's a long walk from the station,' came the firm answer. 'Until four, then. I look forward to meeting you again.'

Two hours later, a rather awed Dot was stepping out of a chauffeur-driven Jaguar, and being shown into the lobby of an imposing block of apartments, overlooking Highgate golf course. Barbara Hescott's apartment was on the eighth floor, and from the wide picture windows you could see right across the golf course to Hampstead Heath beyond. It was furnished on a scale that amply bore out the wealth of its owner, who greeted Dot with a smile holding that by-now-familiar mixture of warmth and irony.

Playing on a carpet in the middle of the lounge was a little dark-haired child, who looked up at Dot, revealing large blue eyes. For a moment the child's mouth opened, as though she was about to speak. She stared at Dot with an intensity that gave Dot a strange prickle of feeling at the back of her neck.

Then she rolled back on to her stomach, apparently absorbed in her game.

Miss Hescott did not introduce Dot to the child. They sat a few feet away, where a silver tray loaded with exquisite china had already been placed, awaiting only a hot teapot.

The first few minutes passed in polite though warm small talk about this and that. On this occasion Miss Hescott was treating her more like a friend than a casual acquaintance.

'I'm going to call you Dorothy,' she said firmly, 'and I want you to call me Barbara, please. We're not in Michael Osborne's stuffy old office now.'

Dot took her cue. 'Miss Hescott—er—Barbara, there's something I have to say straight away.'

'Of course,' said Barbara, as though Dot hadn't spoken, 'her clothes are absurd. Poor Clara, God rest her, had no idea whatsoever.'

Involuntarily, Dot glanced at the child, who was scrawling red circles on a large piece of paper, studiously avoiding looking at Dot. Everything she wore had obviously been bought at some trendy boutique—*haute couture* for kids, rather than practical. The little denims and embroidered blouse were a cut-down version of what a very fashionable adult might have been wearing that autumn, and Dot noticed that the child's ears had been pierced, and that she wore what looked like ruby studs.

She was also noticing that the child was quite exquisitely beautiful; not the conventional prettiness of most little girls, but something quite exceptional. The concentration on the small, oval face seemed to add to its beauty. The large, lustrous eyes were intent on what she was drawing. Checking more closely, though, Dot saw those tell-tale signs of a troubled child, shadows under the eyes and a sulky mouth. Pearl was not sleeping well. But apart from that, the smoothly serene countenance might have served as a model for some Renaissance sculptor carving an angel.

'She loves to draw—adores it. In fact, it's one of the few forms of entertainment I can offer her. I'm not exactly in the way of four-year-olds.'

'She's a lovely child,' Dot said quietly.

'Yes.' A maid had brought tea, and Barbara poured. 'I wanted you to see her, and get to know her a little, before you turned the job down.'

Dot couldn't help smiling. 'How did you know I was going to turn it down?'

'Oh, I think you and I are on the same wavelength, don't you?' Her expression was calm as she passed Dot a cup. 'We've interviewed over forty people, old and young, but none of them even came close, in my opinion. None had that *special* quality which you possess, that light in their eyes that spoke to me, here.' She tapped her heart unselfconsciously. 'Nor did any of them show the genuine concern for the child which you did.'

'Oh!' The wind taken out of her sails, Dot took refuge in tea.

'That's why I wanted your advice. I may have given you the impression that Pearl has scarcely noticed that her mother is gone. Well, that's only partly true. Pearl is used to her mother's absences, because Clara was very far from a devoted parent. But she's starting to cry a lot at night, and she never stops asking when her mummy will come back. I find it very upsetting, and I have no idea what to tell her.' The intelligent brown eyes met Dot's. 'She's too young to grasp a concept like death, isn't she?'

'I would think so. But if she isn't adjusting to the situation, it might be kinder to try and explain to her that her mother is never coming back, rather than to let her keep pining and hoping.'

'My sentiments exactly.' Barbara poured more tea. 'The child is fond of me, in her way. But I'm sixty-eight, Dorothy, and a spinster. I have no touch with children, no knack. I have no idea how to approach this subject. You, on the other hand, will have.'

Dot's eyebrows soared. 'You're not asking *me* to tell the child that her mother isn't coming back?'

'That's exactly what I am asking.'

Dot made a pushing-away gesture with her hands. 'I can't. She doesn't know me from a bar of soap——'

'There's no one else.' The words were dry. 'She has no other relations, and none of Clara's set are worth a damn.'

'Then it's her father's job!'

Barbara shook her head. 'Calum is a brilliant man, but I doubt whether he'd be any better at the job than I would. He hasn't seen much of the child—Clara saw to that. And his own parents died when he was still a baby, so he's not exactly an expert on these things. I would like you to try.'

Dot felt the blood draining from her face. It was the most horribly awkward situation she had been in for a long time. She didn't want to get involved with Pearl, her problems, or her father. It wasn't fair of Barbara to put this pressure on her. She had no right.

'I've been feeling more and more that it's my duty to prepare the child,' Barbara was saying quietly. 'If she accepts that her mother isn't coming back, it will also make her acceptance of Calum so much easier. Otherwise the situation could be awful. And, in the end, it may be better coming from someone she doesn't know yet. Please, Dorothy. I would ask no one else but you.'

Dot looked at the little girl in anguish. At that moment the child got to her feet, and carried her drawing carefully over to where they sat. Without a word, she passed it to Dot.

Dot made out a house, complete with smoking chimney, a bright sun, and three stick figures standing beside it. Dot stared blankly at the eloquent scrawls, then forced herself to smile.

'That's lovely, Pearl. Why don't you colour the sky blue, and the grass green?'

Pearl showed her stumpy red crayon. 'I've only got red.'

'Well, you'll have to ask Auntie Barbara to get you lots of lovely colours.'

The child was looking up at her with an intent expression. 'You were talking about my mummy.'

It wasn't a question, and Dot cursed herself for forgetting how sharp small ears could be. She had thought the child was well out of earshot. She glanced at Barbara, who made a little movement with one hand. 'Yes,' she said slowly to the child, 'we were talking about your mummy.'

Pearl's face was alert. 'When can I go home?'

'You'll be going home very soon,' Dot promised helplessly. Not knowing what else to say, she lifted the little girl on to her knee and cuddled her.

'But you won't be going home to your old place, with all that horrid traffic, and nowhere to play,' said Barbara. 'You'll be going to a lovely *new* house, with a lovely big garden, to stay with your daddy.'

'And my mummy?' Pearl demanded persistently. 'She'll be there, won't she?'

'No, dear.' Barbara's attempt at a softer tone wasn't very successful. 'Your mummy won't be there.'

The child looked up at Dot. 'Do *you* know where she is? When is she coming back?'

'I—I don't know,' stammered Dot, hating herself for her cowardice.

A frown creased Pearl's smooth forehead. 'You said she wasn't coming back.'

'Did I?' Dot hedged, cornered.

'I heard you.'

Oh, damn. *Damn!* Sometimes a child's gaze could pierce you like a searchlight, forcing you to face up to a truth that you wanted to keep hidden. This was her Waterloo. Feeling utterly wretched, Dot smoothed the over-long raven tresses. 'Shall we go for a walk on the Heath?' she suggested with artificial brightness, and met Barbara's eyes briefly. 'We can see if we can catch a butterfly. And I'll try and tell you all about your mummy.'

CHAPTER TWO

EMOTIONAL bonds. Damn them all.

Three weeks later Dot was sitting on the mountainous pile of their suitcases in Tokyo's huge airport, cradling Pearl in her arms. All her troubles, she knew, stemmed from that day on the Heath. From that moment onwards, as Barbara Hescott had very well known she would be, she had been lost, increasingly caught up in her relationship with the child now fast asleep against her breast.

And finally, she had gone against her better judgement, and had taken on a job she had known in her heart was a mistake. The bond with Pearl, forged that afternoon, had ended up dragging her half-way round the world.

The JAL flight from Heathrow had been interminably long, lasting a whole day and a night, and towards the end Pearl had become so wretched with exhaustion and cramp that she had been almost impossible.

Worn out and claustrophobic herself, Dot had been in no mood for tantrums, and had given the child half of one of the sleeping pills the doctor in London had provided her with.

The effects hadn't worn off yet, and mercifully Pearl was still dead to the world.

But where the *hell* was Calum Hescott? She craned around Pearl's tumbled dark head to check her watch. He was over an hour and half late now. They had been sitting here like gypsies, at the International meeting-point, since nine ʻthis morning. The vast crowds

27

hurrying past them in all directions, the incomprehensible babble of Oriental voices, the incessant announcements of flights leaving and flights arriving, were all starting to merge into a nightmarish blur around her. She had long since stopped searching the sea of brown faces for a sight of her employer; it just made her dizzy.

Through the glass walls she could see that the rain was beating down harder than ever, driving with un-European ferocity over the tarmac, making the sky and horizon invisible. The end of September. Monsoon weather. Passengers' feet had tracked wetly all over the floor, adding a depressing touch of squalor to the high-tech impersonality of her surroundings.

She had rung Calum Hescott's home number three times, getting only a Japanese voice, which spoke no English, in reply. Should she ring Barbara?

No. Barbara couldn't do anything from London, and in any case, it was nearly one o'clock in the morning in England now. Damn the man! she thought with a spasm of impotent fury. They had flown across ten time-zones to be here, and he couldn't even be on hand to meet them. Where the hell was he? Hollow-headed with weariness, Dot amused herself by composing all the swear-words she knew into a daisy-chain of rage.

'Dorothy Beech?'

She looked up blankly. A tall man in a rain-slicked mackintosh was looking down at her.

'I'm Calum Hescott.'

She struggled to her feet, her heart suddenly pounding. In her nerves and anger, the daisy-chain of swear-words was threatening to spill out. 'You're nearly two hours late,' she said without preamble, hugging Pearl to her chest and glaring at him.

Eyes that were a deep slaty blue met hers from under a tangle of black hair that was dripping with rain. If she had been expecting apologies, she was to be disappointed. 'Is the kid all right?' asked Calum Hescott.

'She's sleeping. I gave her a pill on the flight.'

His voice was deep, husky. 'What kind of pill?'

'A sleeping pill.'

They stared at one another for a moment. He was a good head taller than Dot, a broad-shouldered man who towered over the diminutive Japanese around them, his body wide and lean, rather than heavy. He was also a fair bit older.

At an initial guess, Calum Hescott was around thirty-six, though his face had a slightly battered look that made his age difficult to guess at. It was a darkly masculine face, the kind of face that would make other men instinctively wary, and that might make some women melt inside. The eyes were remarkably beautiful, darker than Pearl's, and vivid under the dark brows. With the harshly sexy mouth, they were his best feature, for his nose was slightly crooked, as though it had been broken and re-set at some stage.

Dorothy surveyed him in a rather awed silence. Like his hair, his expensive-looking clothes were sodden with rain under the mackintosh, from dusky blue shirt to hand-made leather shoes.

He, for his part, looked less than enchanted with the crumpled appearance Dot presented. He studied her face, her disarranged white linen jacket and her creased yellow dress without enthusiasm. No doubt he expected a woman to look like a Hollywood starlet after twenty hours in an aeroplane, eighteen of them with a child on her lap.

He turned his gaze to the heap of luggage.

'This your lot?'

'Yes.'

'All of it?' he asked drily. 'Touring light obviously isn't your forte.'

'I'm not touring,' she reminded him acidly, 'I'm practically emigrating. And most of it's your daughter's.'

'She must be a budding fashion queen. Wait here, I'll get a trolley.'

Pearl was whimpering, and Dot rocked her in her arms while she awaited Calum's return. Not a very auspicious meeting. Granted, she herself had been snappish, but the last thing he had seemed was pleased to see her.

He was back a short while later with a trolley, which he loaded with an ease that mocked the gasping efforts it had cost her to hump it off the conveyor.

'When will she wake up?' he asked, glancing at Pearl as they headed to the exit.

'An hour or two. Don't expect anything dramatic, though. She's shattered.'

They paused as the doors slid open to bring a rainy gust of wind into their faces.

'Where's your brolly, Mary Poppins?'

'I haven't brought one,' Dot answered irritably, looking out at the sheets of rain sweeping the endless vista of the car park.

'Lesson number one,' he said drily. 'Never come to the land of the rising sun without an umbrella. The car's right over there.'

He hauled off his mackintosh and threw it over both of them like a cape. She felt a muscular arm pull her close with unexpected force, and then he was hustling the three of them, with their bumbling trolley, across the flooded tarmac. The mackintosh kept off the worst of the warm, beating rain, but Dot's feet were still soaked by the time they reached the car. Breathless from carrying Pearl at Calum's merciless pace, she stood by as he unlocked the car.

It was a crimson Porsche sports car, its glamorous lines marred by the large and fresh-looking dent in one front wing. 'That's why I'm late,' he said briefly, nodding at the damage as he let her in.

Sitting in the front seat with Pearl, Dot caught sight of her own face in the rear-view mirror. It was a face that had spent eighteen hours in a jumbo, and it looked tousled, dangerously irritable, and very far from attractive.

She made an effort to smooth her facial topography into something less like a nightclub bouncer's, and shook her dark curls like a wet poodle. Like him or detest him, Calum Hescott was the sort of man who made a woman instantly self-conscious about her appearance.

He slid into the driving-seat and turned to her.

'One thing, just before we set off. I don't want Pearl taking any more pills.'

'What?'

His eyes were hard, like some smoky blue stone. 'I appreciate that the modern woman finds it impossible to cope without a pharmacopoeia of tranquillisers, stimulants and sleeping-pills, but I don't think a four-year-old really needs that kind of aid. So in future, throw them away, or take them yourself.'

'Now just wait a minute, Mr Hescott,' Dot began tightly, as he pulled on his seat-belt.

He turned back to her. 'Yes?'

'I'm not in the habit of taking anything beyond an occasional aspirin, as it happens.' Her voice was unsteady with anger. 'As for the pill I gave Pearl, it was a special children's drug prescribed for her by your aunt's doctor in London. I only gave her a half, and I only gave it to her because she was suffering acutely after fourteen hours in an aeroplane!'

'She was suffering? Or you were suffering?' The sardonic expression was infuriating, but he didn't let her interrupt him. 'I don't want to argue about it. I'm telling you my wishes, and I expect you to obey them.' He reached for the ignition. 'Now, will you put Pearl in the safety-seat, please? It's illegal to carry children in the front seat in Japan.'

'It is in England.'

Gritting her teeth to bite back her anger, Dot lifted Pearl on to the back seat. The perfect father, she thought bitterly, fastening the straps. Pearl was still soundly asleep, and Dot covered her with a rug that Calum silently passed her.

She was too angry even to look at Calum, let alone make small talk. She stared bleakly out at her new world. It was strange, muggy, and very wet. The freeway was choked with horrendous traffic, slowed by the monsoon. Tokyo was a huge grey presence beyond the latticework of steel bridges. Despite the rain, there was a cloud of smog over the city; Manhattan-like skyscrapers rose out of the otherwise featureless sprawl; and when at last she caught sight of Fujiyama to the south-west, it bore no resemblance to the exquisite image of the travel agent's poster. It was just a pale blur in the distance, soon eclipsed by fresh waves of grey, driving rain.

And every face was a Japanese face. Every eye was dark and slanted, everywhere the alien hatchings of Japanese script, on the billboards, on the traffic signals, on the number-plates.

Dot felt a sense of being very far from home start to close in around her, and that, more than anything, made her eventually turn back to Calum. It was time to get back on to the right footing. 'Sorry I was snappish at the airport,' she said with an effort at conciliation. 'I didn't know you'd had an accident.'

'Well, you're not gifted with second sight, are you?'
he replied indifferently. 'It wasn't exactly drastic, but
the Japanese take these things seriously.' He swung out
to take advantage of a gap in the traffic, and for a
moment the smooth power of the car was alarming. No
wonder he had had an accident, Dot thought, clinging
to the seat. 'Know anything about Japan?' he asked,
settling in behind a lorry.

'Only what I've read.'

'Which isn't much?' he suggested sarcastically. She
wanted to retort that she was here for Pearl's sake, not
on a cultural tour, but wisely kept her peace. 'I've done
a little research,' she said neutrally, 'but it's all very new
to me.'

He grunted. 'How's Barbara?'

'She was very well when I left her. She asked me to
pass on her love.'

'She's still planning to come out after Christmas?'

'Yes, at the end of January.' Dot cleared her throat.
'Mr Hescott, perhaps we can have a little talk while your
daughter's asleep?' she suggested.

'In other words, you have something to tell me,' Calum
interpreted. 'Go on, then.'

'It's simply about Pearl's mother. Your ex-wife.'

'Yes, I know who Pearl's mother was,' he said
ironically. 'What about her?'

Dot tried to ignore his manner. 'We—Barbara and I—
decided it was best to try and give Pearl a proper idea
about what's happened, rather than to fob her off with
some pretence.'

Calum glanced at her sharply. 'You've told her that
Clara is dead?'

'Yes.'

'You, personally?'

'Yes.'

'What did she say?'

'She said, "Like the kittens?" I said yes, in a way, but that she'd gone to a beautiful place in the sky, where there weren't any worries or pain, and that she was very happy there.'

Calum had been staring at her so intently that she feared for their safety. Now he looked forward again with a snort. 'I have no idea where Clara has gone to,' he said drily, 'but that's a pretty good description of her general state of mind while she was alive.'

Dot couldn't help being struck by the callous way he said it. There had evidently been little love lost between Calum and Clara Hescott. Would there be any left over for Pearl, she wondered, or would cynicism have poisoned his paternal feelings too? He certainly hadn't shown much sympathy for his motherless little daughter yet. She hoped he wasn't going to use the same abrasive manner towards Pearl. Children responded badly to irony and sarcasm. That was an exclusively adult preserve.

'Well,' Calum said at last, 'the truth is usually better than a lie.'

Glad I've done something right at last, Dot thought, but didn't utter the retort.

'How has she taken Clara's death, generally?'

'She's been through a bad patch,' Dot said bluntly. 'Worse than your aunt imagined, I think—children don't always show their feelings. She still has nightmares, and she talks about her mother a lot, but I think she's accepted that she won't see her again. That means she's coming out of it. Would you consider it presumptuous of me if I made a few suggestions about the way to treat her, for the first couple of days, at least?'

'I assume the handsome salary I'm paying you entitles you to be as presumptuous as you please, so go ahead.'

It wasn't much in the way of invitations, but she went ahead as commanded. It took her half an hour to explain some of the problems that Pearl faced, and some of the solutions that she had found. Calum Hescott listened in silence, driving fast, but with concentration.

Dot studied him as she talked. She was right about the nose; it had definitely been broken, and re-set with a slightly crooked line, but that somehow didn't matter. It suited the rugged heft of his shoulders and arms, and without it the man would have been too handsome for his own good. He was even better-looking than she had given him credit for at first sight. A strong jawline tempered the more seductive features, like the long eyelashes and the dark hair that was now, as it started to dry, showing decisive evidence of a natural curl; and that mouth was, frankly, gorgeous. The kind of mouth that just looking at could make you feel disturbed.

His waist was lean, his legs long and evidently muscular under the rain-blotched denim of his jeans. He looked fit and hard, his strength concentrated in a way that wasted nothing in pointless movement.

All in all, he was a flusteringly attractive man. Yet his manner made every nerve prickle down Dot's spine with antagonism. It wasn't just his sharp way of talking; it was a sense of bitterness in him that darkened his presence, and made her view the coming nine months with something less than enthusiasm.

The sports car was fast, and epitomised a life-style that wasn't exactly cosy. Was there really room in Calum Hescott's life for a recently bereaved four-year-old daughter, complete with governess?

She glanced at him. The lines of his face were very different from Pearl's, yet there was something about the two of them. Certainly, their colouring was identical, but there was something else, perhaps the arrangement of the features, rather than any particular detail, that was unmistakably alike.

Yes, she had it now. Pearl in her most obstinate moods had a look of her father. That moment of frowning sullenness, before the tantrum exploded, was very much Calum's.

Gradually, her little lecture ran down and ground to a halt. He made no comment on her carefully expounded advice, just lapsed into a silence that might have been either indifference or thoughtfulness.

Dot shrugged mentally.

She had said what she wanted to say. He was, by the look of him, a man who liked to make his own mind up; but she hoped he would at least consider what she had told him. Over the past three weeks, she had grown to know Pearl Hescott very well, and to feel very close to her.

She checked on the child, who hadn't stirred. Too tired to bother keeping the conversation going, Dot returned to her contemplation of Japan through the window.

The freeway took them out of the city, and through widely flung suburbs towards the countryside. Now and then the sheets of rain lifted, and between spells Dot got an impression of immaculately neat and well-tended urban perspectives which slowly began to break up, giving way to fields and countryside.

What she could see of the more distant landscape was distinctly rugged, a horizon of rocky mountains and forests, looking as much Alpine as Asian to her untutored eyes.

They pulled off the freeway at last, and drove through a maze of clover-leaf junctions on to a smaller road. Dot gazed at flooded fields and dripping woods, a rocky landscape that now and then changed magically from the banal into something like the Japan of her imaginings.

The buildings were lower than she had expected, with roofs that rose in flat curves to tiled peaks, but the succession of fuel stations and fast-food bars could have been anywhere in America or Europe.

The colours of Japan, however, were subtle. The landscape was as green as England, but the vegetation was very different, the spiky, graceful pines and flourishing clumps of bamboo as different from English broad-leaved trees as the houses were different from English terraces. For the first time, Dot began to get a romantically Eastern feel from her surroundings.

It had stopped raining at last, though the sun was not in evidence. Within a short while they had reached a valley between high peaks.

'This area is called Chinsanzo,' Calum informed her. 'It's where I live.'

'It's very pretty,' Dot said appreciatively. 'Oh, there's a lake!' She stared at the distant grey sheet of tranquil water through rows of pine-trees. This beautiful area was evidently a wealthy residential and holiday zone, for the few houses that could be seen behind their big, well-tended gardens had a grand feel, and here and there was a Western-style hotel, overlooking the lake.

Perhaps Calum found her comments facile, because he didn't respond. But they were soon driving through a gateway and along a drive that led through a rain-washed and wonderful garden, its leaves still dribbling on to the green lawns.

The house was long and low, with a tiled roof. Its already subtle lines were disguised by artful planting so that it seemed to merge into the garden with enchanting modesty. Echoing the lake, there was a large pool in front

of the house, flanked by ancient grey rocks of a formidable size.

Calum parked next to a big clump of ornamental
bamboo, and Dot stepped out, her ears ringing with
weariness and almost twenty-four hours of non-stop
engine noise.

The air was cooler here than in the city, and deliciously fragrant with rain-beaten pine-needles. From
the garden, only the roofs of three or four other houses
could be seen. The rest was a vista of green trees,
stretching out to the still, silvery water. In the distance,
the other end of the lake rose into a sheer, rocky prom-
ontory, where more houses could just be made out,
though disguised far better than any Western houses
would have been in that setting.

Dot lifted Pearl out of the Porsche, and the little girl
began to open her eyes drowsily.

'We're here,' Dot said gently, stroking the black hair
out of her eyes, and followed Calum into the house.

There were three servants to greet them, a man who
hurried off to get the luggage in response to a crackle
of apparently fluent Japanese from Calum, and two
women, one young and one middle-aged, who beamed
at the new arrivals in between a series of deep bows—
and then promptly knelt to unfasten their shoes.

Confounded, Dot replied with a bow of her own,
feeling impossibly tall and gangly before these delicately
proportioned creatures in their plain grey kimonos, who
were deftly trying to slip off her shoes, and offering plain
mule-like sandals in exchange when she resisted.

'This is Oba-san,' said Calum, 'my housekeeper.'

'*Konnichi-wa,*' the housekeeper beamed, managing
another bow from her kneeling position.

'Why does she want my shoes?' Dot asked helplessly.

'The floors inside are *tatami*—rice matting. Wearing your shoes inside a Japanese house is like taking your wellies to bed in England.'

Dot capitulated perplexedly. Even Pearl, it seemed, had to surrender her shoes in exchange for the mules; but Dot was more than grateful to hand her over to Obasan, who perched the little girl on her hip with an expertly motherly air. She seemed to speak a little English, for she bore the child away, asking, 'You like milk? Orange? Coca-Cola?'

Dot walked in, trying to keep the mules on. Her first impression of the house was of beautiful bareness. The floor was of beautifully inlaid wood, for the most part covered with a kind of beige matting, which was firm and comfortable underfoot. Any furniture was minimal, the effect of elegance coming from the restrained harmony of the structures of the house itself.

She turned to Calum, and found that he was hauling off his damp shirt unceremoniously. His naked torso was muscular and tanned, dark male hair etching his chest and stomach. Dot stared, but the younger Japanese woman was apparently unfazed, because she took Calum's shirt quite naturally, and smiled at Dot.

'This is Hanako,' Calum introduced her. 'She speaks a little English, and she understands it well enough.'

'Hello, Hanako,' said Dot.

'Konnichi-wa, Dorote-san,' came the smiling answer.

'Your name is even worse than mine for Japanese tongues,' Calum explained drily. 'The Do-ro bit is easy, but the -thy is impossible. So you're Do-ro-te-san.' He gave Hanako a quickfire order, to which she responded by laughing, nodding, and hurrying away. Her kimono appeared to be fastened by a wide black sash of heavy material, with a large bow-like knot at the back, which caught Dot's bemused attention.

Calum's dark blue eyes met hers, surveying her coolly. He had his aunt's trick of conveying irony by some inner light of his eyes. 'That flight's bloody, isn't it?' he commented.

Dot agreed shortly, not very pleased with what was obviously an observation on her appearance.

'You look like a sleepwalker,' he judged.

'I feel pretty done in.' She tried not to look at his unashamedly beautiful torso. 'I now know what jet-lag is all about!'

'It'll take you a day to recover.' He moved over to her, looking down into her face with hard-eyed interest. 'You look better than you did at the airport, anyway. Almost human, in fact.'

'You're so kind,' Dot said acidly, flushing at the backhanded compliment.

'I think the best thing for you is a bath, a simple meal, and a long, long sleep. How does that sound?'

'Marvellous,' she said with fervour.

He nodded, unsmiling. 'Hanako has gone to prepare the bath. I'll show you your room, and in a little while Hanako will bring your bags and help you unpack. Come.'

Dot followed him in a dreamlike trance with her overnight bag, watching the broad muscles of his naked back. Everything was very alien to her. The doors slid open, rather than swung, and seemed to be made of rectangular wooden frames, covered with paper. Apart from a few pieces of beautiful jade sculpture on carved tables here and there, there was none of the ornamentation or clutter that would have been found in an English house of this size.

Her room was at the end of a long corridor. It had a breathtaking view of the garden and the lake beyond from a wide, low window—but that was about all. The bed was a Japanese-style *futon*, just a flat mattress on the spotlessly clean *tatami* floor, with a crisp white quilt over it. Apart from a row of sliding cupboard doors, and a low, black-lacquered table, there was no other furniture.

A black vase with white and yellow chrysanthemum flowers stood on the table, the only touch of colour or femininity in the room. There were no curtains, no dust, no chairs. The sort of room that looked exquisitely elegant in magazines. But what would it be like to live in?

Calum was watching Dot's blank face with a hint of dry amusement. 'We live in traditional Japanese fashion here,' he told her. 'It might take some getting used to. Don't you like your room?'

She wasn't sure about that, but now was not the time to say so. They could get round to details like that much, much later. Right now, she felt as though she could sleep on a pin, let alone a clean white *futon*. She nodded wearily, and Calum seemed satisfied.

'We're high up here, and it can be chilly at night, especially after rain. If you get cold, Hanako will bring in a heater. You call her Hanako-san, by the way—it's polite. Pearl will be sleeping in the room across the passage. You've got your own washroom through that screen door, and your own patio through that other door. Got your bearings?'

'I think so, Mr Hescott.'

'Calum,' he corrected her. 'And you're Dorothy. Agreed?'

'If you like.'

His eyes held hers. 'Say it, then.'

'Calum,' she repeated in a flat voice.

'Good. See you in a short while.'

He left her to it, and Dot sighed heavily. He didn't like her. Not one little bit.

She looked around, aching to sink into one of the plump, shabby armchairs in her flat. There probably wasn't a plump, shabby armchair for a hundred miles in any direction.

Exploring, she found a spotless little toilet and basin where he had indicated. The cupboard doors, when opened, revealed cavernous space, well laid out in drawers and shelves. Wearily she unclipped her bag and started putting away her things. The alarm clock had to go on the floor, next to her *futon*, as did the half-finished book she was reading. She wondered whether Pearl's room was as bare as this one. And did Calum himself sleep in a room like this?

There was a tap on her door, which then slid open to reveal Hanako and the manservant, with her three suitcases.

When the man had retired, she and Hanako unpacked, the little Japanese moving with fluent, quick gestures as she obeyed Dot's pantomime indications. It took only a few minutes to put away Dot's cut-down wardrobe, and at last she wryly surveyed the filled cupboard. Well, she was here, and here she was. Nine months of Japan and Calum Hescott ahead of her.

She turned to Hanako.

'Thank you so much. What is "thank you" in Japanese?'

'*Arigato gozaimasu.*'

'*Arigato gozaimasu*, Hanako-san.'

'Pleasure!'

They exchanged bows, which sent Hanako into a fit of giggles, putting her hand in front of her mouth. 'Where is Pearl, the little girl?'

'Pearl-san with Oba-san now.' Hanako mimed eating and sleeping, then folded her hands with a smile. 'Bath ready now, Dorote-san. You like come?'

'Oh, yes, please.'

Hanako got a towel and Dot's robe ready, then bustled round Dot to start unfastening the zip of her dress.

'Do I have to take my clothes off here?' Dot asked in perplexity. Hanako nodded briskly, and Dot allowed the girl to help her undress, reflecting that the taste of Japan she had had so far was very strange indeed.

Hanako reacted to Dot's nudity with the same indifference as she had to Calum's stripping off of his shirt. Trying not to make any prudish or gauche mistakes, Dot belted the gown around herself, and followed Hanako out of the room.

She was led through the house and across a tiny covered courtyard to a building that resembled a very large sauna. It was so filled with steam that Dot's gown clung to her body instantly. Within, she could just make out a huge sunken bath, the size of a small pool, set round with flat paving. The steam had a not unpleasant mineral smell, and hot water was trickling constantly into the bath from a prettily arranged stone waterfall in one corner, set around with luxuriant ferns and bromeliads.

All this, for her? Talk about luxury!

Hanako helped her off with her gown, then bowed her way out of the bath-house, closing the door.

Dot paused on the edge, naked, to tie her hair up. The damp weather was making it curl furiously. Was it Japanese etiquette to wash your hair in the bath? she wondered. She had no soap or shampoo. Well, a soak would do wonderfully for the time being.

Her figure was slender, tall for a woman, with nothing heavy about it. Her breasts were small and high, tipped with delicate pink, and her legs were long and slim. Standing there, she might have been a sculpture in creamy Parian marble, until she moved, padding gingerly down a set of stone steps, and dipping a foot in the water.

'Ouch!' It was fiercely hot.

'Forty-seven degrees centigrade.' The deep, lazy voice drifted out of the steam. 'It comes out of the rock at that temperature, and we channel it into the bath-house with pipes.'

Dot's hands had flown to cover her vital areas at the first words. Now, with horror, she realised that Calum Hescott was already in the water, lying against the opposite side, his muscular arms outstretched. He considered her age-old pose through the steam, his eyes glinting with irony.

'*Venus Surprised Bathing*. Or perhaps, *Diana after the Hunt*. Get in, Mary Poppins, and stop posing for a Pre-Raphaelite painting.'

Without thinking, Dot slid straight into the water, gasping as the intense heat enveloped her. The bath, which had a smooth rock floor, was only waist-deep, and she had to crouch for modesty.

Damn him! she thought in disbelief. He had been lying there while she stripped, watching her as she had stood on the edge, doing her hair and mooning like an idiot.

She was trying to formulate some blistering reproof, but the heat and her tiredness were making her thoughts wobble dizzily.

'What—what—the hell are you doing here?' she puffed.

'Taking a bath. Like you.'

She was still trying to recover from the combined shock of the heat and finding herself sharing a bath with an obviously naked Calum. Hanako had abandoned her, and she was all alone with him. For the first time she noticed his deep blue robe, neatly folded over a rock. 'You might have told me you were going to be here,' she said angrily. 'I wouldn't have dreamed of coming if I'd known you were in here!'

'Why not?'

'I'm not in the habit of giving free peep-shows to strange men!'

Calum's eyes narrowed. 'Peep-shows? You think highly of your endowments, Miss Poppins. If I wanted to gawk at naked femininity, I would look elsewhere than my daughter's governess. In any case,' he drawled, 'I rather think I prefer the Japanese variety of nudity. A woman naked and relaxed is beautiful. A woman naked and ashamed is just embarrassing.'

Dot glared at him, speechless. He was holding a sort of bamboo ladle, which he pointed at her. 'You're going to have to leave your Western ideas about nudity behind,' he advised calmly. 'They have no place in Japan. Communal bathing is a fact of life here.'

'Not for me!' The water was spreading its ruthless heat between her thighs, across her breasts and stomach. 'I happen to be an Englishwoman.'

He examined her ironically. 'A very pink Englishwoman. Are you feeling all right?'

'It's terribly hot,' she panted, her forehead damp with perspiration. She eyed him cautiously, praying he would keep his distance. 'You can't be serious! This is where people wash? Together?'

'Not wash,' he corrected her. 'Bathe. You should have washed before you came in here. There's a bath and shower just opposite your room. This is something else entirely.'

'You're damned right it is,' Dot muttered grimly.

'The minerals in the water are very good for you. They'll wash away the bad effects of your journey—and the bad effects of my crash.' He pointed at the waterfall. 'That comes from a volcanic spring in my garden. It's one of the reasons why I bought the property in the first place.' He rose to his feet, his wet body magnificent, and waded towards her. She was mesmerised by the way the crisp black hair streaked wetly down his flat, muscular belly. Through the shimmering green water she could see the darker shadow of his loins, and she turned her back on him hastily, hugging her small, neat breasts. Her own pale body was all too visible in the clear water.

'The Japanese,' he said from behind her, 'aren't ashamed of their bodies.' He dipped the bamboo ladle into the water, and trickled a stream of water over her shoulders. 'Nor should you be. If you were old and fat, it would be understandable. Considering that you're neither, and have an acceptable figure...' the ladle poured hot water down the back of her neck, and she felt his fingers caress her nape soothingly, '...shame is inappropriate. This is a country where mental privacy is important, but physical privacy is not. Mixed bathing has no sexual connotations. Men and women do it together all over Japan, without a moment of prurience or embarrassment.'

'But we're not Japanese—we're both English! You can't expect me to just forget all the conventions I've grown up with!'

'You're not in England any more,' he reminded her. 'You're in my bath, in Japan.'

'I'm too hot,' panted Dot, twisting away from the seductive caress. 'I want to get out.'

'Get out, then,' Calum said impatiently. 'I'm not keeping you.'

She stared at the steps despairingly. How was she ever going to get out of this cauldron and keep her dignity intact? 'Turn your back, then!'

He snorted in contempt. 'I can't believe this is the same woman who droned so solemnly and sensibly at me all the way here in the car. Does nudity really have such a disruptive effect on your thinking?'

She faced him, feeling another wave of dizziness sweep across her mind. 'I don't think this is right,' she said, forcing her voice to sound brisk. 'I'm going to be Pearl's governess, and unless you treat me correctly from the start, my work here is going to be a complete failure!'

He was watching her, his lids heavy over those beautiful, smoky blue eyes. A slight smile curved his mouth. 'Your *work*? Your extended paid holiday, you mean.'

'That's an extraordinary thing to say!'

'The truth is stranger than fiction, so I'm told.'

Dot pressed her palms to her burning cheeks and stared at him. 'Don't you have any respect for my professional capacity?'

'Not much,' he said with an easy contempt that shocked her.

'Then you could at least show some minimum regard for my privacy, my feelings, or even my—or even my womanhood!'

'Your womanhood?' He smiled slightly, and tossed the ladle to the side, tanned muscles shifting in his arms and chest. 'You're supposed to be relaxing in the spring water, and getting your *yin* and *yang* into balance, not thinking about your womanhood. You're a very uptight lady, Miss Poppins.'

'Stop calling me Miss Poppins!' she snapped. She was breathless with the heat, her emotion, and his proximity. 'You're deliberately setting out to humiliate me!'

He stared at her. Those slate-blue eyes were hard to meet; there was something so blatantly assessing about them that they made her heart turn over inside her. He looked at women in the way an ancient Roman would have considered a naked slave-girl he was thinking of buying.

'Barbara led me to expect something special from you,' he said quietly, 'but I don't see anything special at all, Dorothy-san. Not so far.' The wet sheen of steam made his body gleam like freshly poured bronze. 'In any case, you're way off beam. It's true I may not have much respect for your professional capacity. But your womanhood is something quite different.' He smiled mockingly. 'Especially when it's displayed to such delicious effect at the edge of my bath.'

'What do you mean? I don't see how you can be so snide about my professional status,' she retorted angrily. 'What have I done to make you despise me?'

'If you're going to yell at me you'd better get out of this water, or you'll burst something.' He waded towards the steps, and got out. Dot averted her gaze hastily as he emerged from the steamy water, and found herself glaring at the scalding waterfall. Her blood felt as though it were literally boiling. It was hot, so very hot; the steam was making her eyelids heavy, making her head and back of neck throb.

'It isn't good for you to have bad emotions in honourable volcanic spring water.'

She looked mutinously over her shoulder. He was wearing his robe now, and holding her robe out.

'Come on,' he commanded wearily, 'get out.'

'Not with you standing there!' But a wave of giddiness swept across her mind. The throbbing was becoming a pounding in her blood. She was a block of ice in this fiercely alien heat, and if she didn't escape soon she would melt away to nothing. She had to get out, she had no option.

Biting her lip, she waded leadenly over to where Calum waited and emerged from the water, reaching as hastily as she could for her towelling robe.

Calum wrapped it round her, and stared down at her damp face. 'Are you all right?'

'I don't feel very well,' she gritted. 'Can I go outside?'

'Best cool down gradually in here,' he advised. 'You were stupid to get all excited like that. The water's marvellously beneficial, but only if you relax in it.' There was a jug of orange juice on a bamboo tray, and he poured her a small glassful. 'Sip that.'

Dot obeyed, feeling horribly weak. The air was so steamy, it was hard to breathe.

'You have beautiful eyes,' murmured Calum, watching her dispassionately. 'Grey and clear, like amethysts.'

There was a roaring in her ears. She managed to put the glass down without dropping it, but the movement made the world spin around her wildly. She reached instinctively for Calum's strong shoulders to stop herself from falling.

'Hey,' he said gently, his arms moving around her, 'take it easy.'

But the roaring was swelling. The darkness was filling her mind. She clung to him tightly, trying to tell him she was going to faint. Her tongue would not obey.

Her thoughts reeled. Where was she? A deathly giddiness had her in its grip, and the darkness had grown to obliterate everything, making her call out, 'Calum!' like a drowning woman, as she sank like a stone into the darkness that was waiting for her.

CHAPTER THREE

IT WAS cool on the *futon*, the crispness of the white quilt comforting against Dot's naked skin. But the mattress was far harder than she was used to, and she rolled on to the other side, feeling the bones of one hip start to throb.

The movement brought her drowsy mind closer to wakefulness. The waiting memories insinuated themselves into her thoughts. Instantly, heat flooded her cool white world.

That awful faint by the pool. The total blackness followed by confused memories of being carried by Calum, slack-limbed and helpless, into the house.

The clucking of Oba-san and Hanako over her limp form, Calum's strong hands patting her naked body dry with a cool towel, then depositing her in her bed. Her own feeble moaning throughout the performance...

It was all too humiliating for words. Dot crushed her face against the hard little pillow, bunching her fists. What a mean, cruel trick to play on her! It occurred to her that Calum Hescott was the only man who had ever seen her naked like that, certainly the only man who had ever watched her as she stood, doing her hair, without a stitch on.

And he held her in contempt—had told her so, with no compromises.

She sat up, raking her fingers through the tangle of her hair.

It was evening, the last vestiges of the sunset ragged in the sky through her window. By the alarm clock beside her, she had been asleep for eight hours. Physically, she felt stiff and gritty-eyed, but that was nothing to her mental bruises.

She rose stiffly and pulled on her robe. The mirror in her little wash-room revealed shadows under her grey eyes, and a bruised look to her mouth.

She washed her face with cold water, her mind full of grim thoughts. She had to set this situation straight, if that were possible, without any delay. It was impossible to continue on this basis, without the trust and respect of her employer. Nine long months stretched ahead, and this had been a very poor beginning.

She must see Pearl, and find out how she was. By this hour, especially after such a long journey, she ought to be tucked up safely in bed. Heaven knew what had been happening while she had slept the afternoon away. What a day! What a start to her life in Japan.

She dressed in denims and a long-sleeved shirt, pulling on a white mohair jersey against the evening chill, and brushed her hair into some semblance of order. Her nature rebelled against make-up, but her face looked so pale and wan that she reluctantly added a touch of lipstick and rouge, then went in search of Pearl.

The sound of distant laughter led her down the corridor, to a set of wide sliding doors, the transparent rectangular panes glowing with a soft light from within. She could hear Pearl's voice, high and excited from inside, and the deeper murmur of her father.

Gathering her courage, she pushed the doors aside on their tracks and stepped into the room.

A small fire was burning in a simple grate in one corner. Its warm glow spread through the room. In front of the grate, on the inevitable *tatami* matting, Calum Hescott sprawled on his back among a welter of cushions, holding Pearl in the air above him. He was wearing a dark grey *kimono*, his muscular, tanned forearms emerging from the wide sleeves to support the little girl, who was gurgling with delight.

'And *then*,' he was saying in a fierce growl, 'the woodsman *chopped* the wicked wolf up with his great big axe—and *who* was inside?'

'The granny!' Pearl crowed in delight.

'Red Riding Hood's granny,' Calum confirmed, rolling over on to one side and plonking her on to her bottom. 'Safe and sound, and only missing her false teeth.'

Dot felt her heart melting at the scene. At last little Pearl had a father to tell her fairy-tales. Pray heaven this wasn't the spoiling that usually had, as its other side, neglect and indifference.

Then she recognised the hectic pink in Pearl's cheeks. It was definitely her bedtime, before a storm of exhausted tears ended the fun.

'There's Dorothy!' cried Pearl, catching sight of Dot's still figure. She scrambled to her feet and ran over to Dot's arms. 'Daddy wouldn't let me wake you,' she declared, looking up with bright blue eyes. 'He said you were sleeping. Did you sleep *all* afternoon?'

'I'm not a little rubber ball, like you,' Dot smiled. 'Long journeys take it out of me. Have you been awake *all* afternoon?'

'Yes! Daddy's been telling me stories!'

'I see.' Dot walked towards the fire, where Calum was now sitting up, one lean hand grasping his other wrist around his upraised knees. She met his eyes coldly. 'Hello, Calum.'

'Hello, yourself. How do you feel?'

'I feel fine, thank you,' she said formally. 'But it's past eight. Time for Pearl to get washed and go to sleep.'

Pearl squealed in dismay, raising an imploring face to Dot.

'Have a heart,' Calum said easily. 'It's her first night in Japan, and I haven't seen her for months.'

'She's here to stay,' Dot reminded him coolly. 'She'll be available tomorrow. And she'll be worn out after the flight, especially as you've been amusing her all afternoon. She may not show it, but she needs her rest. Come on, Pearl.'

'No!' Pulling her hand out of Dot's, Pearl ran over to her father and clambered on to his knee for refuge, looking at Dot defiantly over one shoulder. Calum's arms wrapped round the child, and he looked drily at Dot across the Pearl's head. 'You're out-voted, it seems,' he observed.

Did he think it was amusing to challenge her authority like this? She glanced at the child's over-bright eyes. 'Pearl,' she said quietly, 'it's your bedtime. Come on.'

'She doesn't want to sleep yet. What are you going to do?' Calum asked drily. 'Feed her another sleeping tablet?'

Dot bit down her anger. 'She'll sleep without that, don't worry. Pearl's exhausted. She has too much stamina for her own good.' She lifted her voice. 'Pearl, you know you're worn out. Come *now*.'

For a moment she thought that rebellion would break out. But three weeks of Dot's company had forged a bond that was too strong to break just yet.

Reluctantly, Pearl emerged from the fortress of Calum's arms and trudged over to Dot. 'Good girl,' said Dot, hiding her relief. 'Say goodnight to Daddy. Now,' she invited, when a reluctant kiss had been given, 'why don't you show me where your bedroom is?'

She felt Calum's eyes boring into her back as she walked out with Pearl. Time enough to deal with *him* later.

Pearl's bed, too, was a *futon*, a cut-down version with pink polka-dots. Toys were scattered all over the floor, and there was a giant panda in one corner, obviously a gift from Calum.

Fifteen minutes took care of the undressing, washing and teeth-cleaning ceremonies, and about fifteen seconds in the bed took care of Pearl's remaining stock of consciousness. She slept like an angel, clutching her favourite rag doll.

Leaving the tiny nightlight on, Dot emerged from the little bedroom, to find Calum leaning against the opposite wall. His expression was not warm.

'I'm going to have a whisky,' he said. 'What will you have?'

It was a command, rather than an invitation. 'Fruit juice,' said Dot, 'if you have any.'

'Fruit juice. I suppose a paragon like you never touches alcohol?'

'Very seldom, actually.'

He nodded, and led the way back to the fire.

There was nowhere to sit except on the floor, among the cushions. Dot curled up in a little nest by the fireside, feeling she was in for a confrontation in a minute or two.

'This is guava,' he said, holding out a glass of pink fruit juice. 'It's fresh.'

The thick, icy drink was strange but delicious. Calum sank to the floor next to her with a glass of amber liquid. He looked at his ease in that position. No wonder he preferred the loose Japanese kimonos; tight denims were not designed for sitting around on the floor in.

'Sorry if I came the heavy governess just now,' Dot began without preamble, 'but it's taken me some effort to get her to keep to a regular bedtime. She was in the habit of going to sleep and getting up at all hours, and

I don't want her getting back to her bad old ways, not even on a special occasion like this one.'

He drained half the glass. 'You really take it seriously, don't you, this governess bit?'

'It's my job,' she pointed out brightly. What the hell did he think she was here for? 'I would like her to be in bed every night before eight o'clock,' she went on, trying not to sound too bossy. 'Early nights have done her such a lot of good already.'

'Well, they tell me you're an expert,' he said coolly. 'I'll see that Oba-san gets the message.'

'Oh, don't worry Oba-san. I'll put her to bed myself.'

'My housekeeper has four children and three grand-children,' said Calum with unmistakable irony. 'I think she's capable of taking care of Pearl's bedtime. And she won't need sleeping pills to get Pearl to sleep, either.'

Dot winced.

'She'll also supervise Pearl's bathtime, and will make sure she gets a proper diet—she's a very talented and experienced cook.' His look silenced Dot's interruption. 'Hanako will take care of dressing the child, brushing her hair, and so forth.'

Dot took a deep breath. 'I don't want to seem argu-mentative, but there really is no need for your servants to take care of Pearl's bathtime, or anything else. I'm here to do all that. I'd prefer to do it, in fact. It will help me establish and maintain a bond with Pearl.'

The dark eyes gleamed with what might have been anger. 'And what if I don't want you to establish and maintain bonds with my daughter?'

'I beg your pardon?' said Dot, taken aback.

He spoke clearly and quietly. 'I said, supposing I don't what you playing surrogate mother to my daughter?'

The crooked nose made his face almost frightening when he wore that particular look. Dot felt a cold chill

prickle down her back. She hadn't realised just how unwelcome she was here. This could be a very awkward
situation indeed.

'I'm a surrogate mother only in a very limited sense,
Mr Hescott. A governess doesn't usually go beyond
teaching, but in the case of a child of this age——'

'Governess,' Calum cut in, draining his glass. 'Funny,
I've never liked that word. It has an ugly ring to my
ears, a cold, prissy sound to it.'

She met the challenge of his eyes briefly. 'I'm not cold,
and I'm not prissy.' She picked her words carefully. 'As
a governess, my main concern is Pearl's education. I'm
fully qualified to teach pre-school children, and I can
make sure Pearl's mind gets all the stimulation it needs
over the next nine months. I can teach her to read and
write, just for one thing—not to mention some basic
manners, which is just as important. If you insist that
I don't deal with your daughter's dressing and washing,
then of course I won't. But I do feel it would be better
if I did.'

'You do?' The V of his kimono revealed a muscular
throat, and the start of crisp, dark curls that, she knew,
covered his chest. He was watching her with eyes the
colour of a stormy sky. 'Why? So that you can mon-
opolise my daughter's attention?'

'Just the opposite, actually.' Why did she feel as
though she were on trial? 'You have your work. You
can't be with her every minute of the day, and nor can
Hanako or Oba-san—they've got their duties too. I can
be with her, though. It's my job to be with her, and by
signing that contract in London I've dedicated the next
nine months of my life to your daughter. I'd like to do
my job properly, not for anyone's sake except Pearl's.'

'In other words, to get back to what I said earlier,
you want to play Mum to the orphaned tot.'

Dot put her glass down, feeling anger ignite inside her. 'I don't see any necessity for that tone. Why did you ask Barbara to advertise for a governess, if you didn't want one?'

Calum's eyes were emotionless. 'The idea was Barbara's, not mine.'

'Barbara's?'

'There's a popular prejudice against single fathers. Haven't you noticed? Any judge will always award custody to the mother, no matter whether she's patently incapable of looking after a toy poodle, let alone a child.' His mouth, normally mobile and passionate, was a bitter slash. 'Even my revered aunt Barbara seems to feel I'm inadequate to look after Pearl on my own. She insisted that a female presence was necessary. I disagreed. I didn't want you here, I didn't want anyone. In my view, Oba-san and Hanako are quite adequate to care for Pearl. You're a product of my aunt's preconceptions.'

'I hadn't realised you felt that way,' she said in a remote voice. 'May I ask how you intended to oversee your daughter's education?'

'There's an excellent school for under-fives not three miles from here.'

'An English-language school?'

'No. But I assure you that Pearl will pick up two hundred words of Japanese in the time it takes you to pick up two dozen. Children absorb languages very quickly.'

'Yes, but Pearl is an English child——'

'She may have to spend several years more in Japan,' Calum cut through. 'I like it here. I've bought this house, and the company I work for are very keen to renew my contract. They pay me very well, I can assure you. I speak the language, and I'm in no hurry to leave. The idea of sending an overpaid English governess out here to insulate my daughter from Japanese culture is, frankly, repugnant to me.

'I see.' Dot was hardly convinced by his assumption that Pearl didn't need someone of her own culture to care for her, but she was wise enough not to say so.

'As for what you call establishing and maintaining bonds with Pearl, that's something which I find even more repugnant. It strikes me as a very dangerous thing to do. You're not Pearl's mother, and your time here is strictly limited. Very probably, you won't even see out your nine-month contract.'

'I see,' Dot said again, her mouth dry.

'I don't want Pearl's emotions torn any more than they have been, which will inevitably happen when you leave. No doubt you're used to such partings, and your exorbitant salary must cushion the shock very nicely. But Pearl isn't getting anything on the deal. So just what do you have on offer, Mary Poppins? Apart, that is, from putting my daughter to bed every night at what you deem an appropriate hour?'

Dot swallowed. There was something about the hard cynicism of that harshly beautiful face that made her feel hopelessly out of her depth. It didn't help to keep remembering that those hard blue eyes had seen her naked a few hours ago, either.

'I'm not going to take offence at your remarks,' she told him quietly, 'even though they were deeply offensive. You're right, of course. My coming into Pearl's life at this time is fraught with emotional problems. I realised that at once.' She changed her position, cursing the lack of any kind of easy chairs. She didn't have Calum's ability to sit motionless on the *tatami*, and her legs were all pins and needles. 'I made exactly these objections to Barbara when she talked me into the job.'

'Barbara talked you into it?' he queried cynically.

'Oh yes,' Dot nodded, her clear grey eyes meeting his without flinching, 'she talked me into it, Mr Hescott. I didn't want to get into this situation either, any more than you did. But your aunt's viewpoint was that Pearl needed a friend, a mother-substitute, as you like to put it, very urgently.'

You're not keen on the job, and I quite understand why. I'm not going to beat about the bush, Dorothy. I want you for Pearl. Pearl needs you. Dot could hear Barbara's words now. She was remembering something else Barbara had said, after that afternoon on the Heath:

I won't disguise my nefarious scheme. I'm hoping to be able to change your mind, and I hope that Pearl is going to help me do that. And I hope you'll stick with her, no matter what obstacles come in your way.

She met Calum's eyes, who was looking at her measuringly. This was an obstacle she hadn't anticipated!

'In her opinion, Pearl needed a woman's care.' She felt her cheeks colour slightly. 'A woman's love, to put it more accurately. And in her present situation, even temporary love is better than no love at all.'

'Ah.' His jaw tightened. 'I'm not capable of giving her love, then?'

'You can give her a father's love. I can give her—well, if not a mother's love, then at least a woman's love. I'm here for Pearl's sake,' she told him firmly, 'not because I wanted the exorbitant salary, or because I thought I was getting a free holiday in Japan.'

His face was brooding. 'So you had to be bribed into coming here?'

'Why do you always jump to the worst conclusions? Pearl has had a tragic shock, and of course, she'll feel the effects for a long time to come. That's something I think I can help her with. Becoming a substitute mother is a very crude way of putting it, but there is some truth in that description. If I am a substitute mother, however, it will only be until Pearl is able to forge a proper bond with you. My influence over her ought to grow less and less. In the meantime, I can provide a kind of link. I'm always here, someone who speaks her language and shares her culture. That may not seen much to you, but I think it will mean a great deal to Pearl.'

Dot rose to her feet and looked down at Calum.

'There isn't much else I can say. I recognise the difficulties, and I'll do my best to avoid them, if I can. There's been a certain amount of sacrifice involved on my part already, and I don't expect the next nine months to be roses either. If you want to cancel that contract and send me home again, then you're welcome to do so. As long as you pay my expenses, I don't care whether I never see you—or Japan again.'

Calum rose too. He came close, and took her chin in his hand, tilting her face up so that he could look into her eyes. His dark stare seemed to reach into her mind, making her feel invaded, helpless.

'You're a very articulate young lady,' he said softly, not taking his eyes away from hers. 'No, I won't send you back—not yet. But you're costing me a fortune, Mary Poppins, and I begrudge every penny you're costing me. So you'd better damned well *earn* every penny, or it will give me great pleasure to do exactly as you've just invited me to do.'

He released her chin, and Dot took a step back, her cheeks bright with colour.

'I'll do the best job I can,' she said tightly.

Calum smiled without humour, and drained the rest of his glass.

'You can have your way about caring for Pearl for a fortnight. If I don't like the way things are going, I'll tell you.'

'Very well.'

'Now, before you get another fit of the vapours, we'd better get some food into you. You must be hungry.'

'Very,' she said, and then remembered her conversation with Susie about food.

He caught the wary look in his eyes. 'Since you disapprove of Japanese bathing habits, Japanese beds, and Japanese footwear, I take it you're not ready for raw fish and bean-curd?'

'I'd settle for a boiled egg.'

'Come on, then,' he said brusquely, walking away, 'I'll show you where the kitchen is. Oba-san has the night off on Fridays, so we're left to our own devices.'

The kitchen, at least, was thoroughly modern, and equipped with every electronic sophistication. The other side of Japan, she reflected, as she watched Calum make them a meal of scrambled eggs, mushrooms and bacon, American-style, using the microwave, a blender, and an electric grill. They spoke little, and the few words they had were not conversation, just necessary exchanges of information.

While waiting for her meal, Dot was trying to digest the very indigestible mental lump she had just had to swallow.

She watched his tanned, uncompromisingly male face, with its disfigured nose and devastating mouth.

One slip of any kind, and she could expect to be out.

It was not the ideal working environment, and if Calum's hostility towards her was picked up by Pearl, she would find it very hard to keep any kind of trusting relationship with the child. Especially if Calum started challenging her decisions in front of Pearl...

The thought made her wince inwardly. If she was lax about her job from now on, which was hardly in her nature, Calum would be justified in sending her away as a waste of money. But if she was too zealous, and clashed with his probably over-indulgent ideas of what was best for his daughter, she would be dismissed as a nuisance.

Oh, damn... Why was this job so fraught with problems?

'One Japanese custom you'll definitely have to assimilate are these.' He held up a pair of slender black chopsticks. 'If you can't use them, you're going to look like a savage whenever we eat out, or have friends for a meal.'

Dot groaned mentally, but tried to look interested. He took her right hand and pushed the smooth sticks into the right places, showing her how to manipulate them correctly. His touch was firm and warm, and for some reason, the colour mounted to Dot's cheeks.

'I think I've got it,' she said stiffly, snapping the chopsticks clumsily.

'The one thing to avoid is shovelling food into your mouth with them. That's for children and barbarians.' He served up the food, laying the portions neatly on black plates. 'You pick up little bits, and lift them to your mouth.'

'How do you tackle something like steak?' Dot wanted to know, chasing a mushroom round her plate.

'Most dishes come ready cut in bite-sized pieces.' He was watching her performance with ironical eyes. 'Japanese chefs pride themselves on the sharpness of their kitchen knives.'

Dot struggled to get the food down before it cooled, hunger battling with clumsiness. He, on the other hand, ate with deftness, not bothering to hide his contempt for her lack of dexterity.

It's not you, she told herself. He would have been as hostile with anyone who had arrived to fill the post.

'For heaven's sake,' he sighed, and leaned over to take the chopsticks out of her fingers. 'Like this. Watch.'

He picked up a button mushroom and lifted it to her mouth. She opened her lips hesitantly, and he popped the morsel in, making her feel as gauche as Pearl. She was pink-cheeked again as he slotted the chopsticks back into her hand, and let her get on with it.

He made her feel so awkward. The truth was that she was very unused to men, let alone men like Calum Hescott. She had never, despite her beauty and poise, got over her inner shyness with members of the opposite sex.

Dot had once been badly hurt by an older man called Jack Taunton, who had played with her heart in a way that had left bruises there, bruises that had taken a long time to heal.

Since Jack, there had been a reserve in her which had left more than one boyfriend baffled, and once or twice had resulted in the dark mutter, 'Frigid!'

But she wasn't frigid. She was a virgin, it was true, and at twenty-five that wasn't usual these days. But she was aware of strong sexual feelings inside herself. Like all women, she sometimes ached for physical love.

It was simply that Mr Right had never come along, with the right key to her particular lock. She had thought that Jack Taunton was Mr Right, but things hadn't worked out, and he had left her painfully hurt and confused. The only thing that had saved her from even worse hurt was that she had never entered a physical relationship with Jack; and that lesson had stuck with her.

In any case, promiscuity was not possible for her. She valued herself too much, and she had too many intimate dreams about sex and love to want to squander them on an affair with someone who didn't care, deep down, where it mattered.

So, for all her cool equilibrium, she was never at her ease with men. And when it came to a man handsomer than any she had ever met, and with a dark, animal sexuality that seemed to throb in the air, she was aware of alarm bells going off all over her body.

In a sense, his hostility helped keep things on an even keel, because without that she suspected she would be a blushing, clumsy disaster area. As it was, her efforts with the chopsticks were so dismal that Calum eventually took scornful pity on her, and passed her a plastic spoon.

'Just this once, Miss Poppins.'

With which degrading implement Dot finished her by now cold meal.

She wasn't impressing him. She wasn't making any kind of impression at all.

He had even stopped mocking her now, and when he eventually said he had work to do in his study, and bade her goodnight, the atmosphere was one of a chilly politeness.

She peeped in at Pearl, who was still fast sleep in the same position, then made her way back to her own room, feeling wretched about the day and its events. She undressed, and tried to escape into the pages of her book. But the fictional happenings had lost their appeal for her, and she settled, after a few listless pages, for an early night.

A slight shower had started. She lay in the darkness, listening to the raindrops spatter among the leaves outside, bringing the cool, piny scent of Japan into her bedroom, and thought about the train of events that had led her here.

Barbara, she felt sure, had known exactly how Calum would receive her, but for one reason or another had let her walk into the bear-trap unforewarned. Far from the general situation, where her services were welcomed, and her company was appreciated, she would be living here in a state of wary probation, over-conscious of every clumsiness, every error she committed.

Would it have been different, she wondered, if she'd turned out to be a middle-aged dragon, like the ones she'd seen in Michael Osborne's office that day? Perhaps it was her youth that made Calum so derisive of her?

She had meant to tell him off about the way he had humiliated her over the bath episode, but somehow it hadn't seemed an appropriate topic.

She must have still owed her mind a debt of sleep, because her thoughts soon drifted into the gentle flickering of dreams.

Just before true sleep came, she thought she felt strong fingers touch her chin, and heard a deep voice in her mind. 'You have beautiful eyes. Grey and clear, like amethysts.'

She half woke, her heart beating. She had forgotten *that* little comment until now. Calum had made it just before she had fainted into his arms.

Had she really fainted in his arms? She shuddered. No, today hadn't gone very well at all. Dot rolled over, relaxing her mind.

Dorothy's first two weeks at Chinsanzo were a process of fitting into the routines of the household, and establishing routines of her own with Pearl. She asked Calum to set aside a teaching-room, which he did with unmistakable irony, and there she started reading and writing lessons at once, finding Pearl a quick and eager learner.

Living in a Japanese house required considerable adaptation at first.

In his two years here, Calum had assimilated the Japanese life-style perfectly, and he wasn't amused by

Dot's early errors, like the time she tried to push a door open, and found she had thrust her hand through a paper panel.

Or the time she forgot to change Pearl's shoes after a walk out in the wet, and the child left muddy footprints across the spotless beige *tatami*, a mishap which reduced Oba-san to squeaks of horror.

But gradually Dot started to appreciate the spare beauty of the house, and its superb garden. The clean, lucid lines of the house brought great peace to a tense mind, which was no doubt why Calum had opted for a thoroughly Japanese way of life.

He did a lot of his work at home, designing with the aid of specialised computers in his vast, uncluttered study. Usually he went to the Tokyo office in the mornings, but he was often home in the afternoons.

Dot found she could always tell when he was in. The whole atmosphere of the house altered. When Calum-san was home, the two women servants hurried about their tasks with happy faces and eager steps.

The Japanese world, Dot had realised with more than one sigh, was definitely a man's world.

Hanako would just giggle if she ruined one of Dot's silk shirts by putting it through the hot cycle of the washer. But let Calum remark that the *kobe* beef was too salty, and there would be tears in the kitchen. She had seen it happen.

She wondered drily how Calum would adjust when he moved back to a world where women were less accustomed to subservience!

As Barbara had predicted, Calum's social life was busy. He played squash three times a week at the sports club down by the lake, the explosive exercise no doubt helping to keep that formidably muscled body in trim.

He was regularly out for what were called 'working lunches' or 'business evenings'. The latter usually went on until the small hours, and Dot had heard the words 'geisha house' mentioned several times in connection with them. Though Oba-san assured her that they were very cultured places, Dot's mind formed a lurid picture of what went on, filling her with rather shocked disapproval.

Well, Calum Hescott was a single man, and a very masculine one. Most of the women among his friends were married. If he went to geishas with his men friends, who was she to disapprove? He clearly needed some kind of dissipation to counteract the good effects of the squash.

And from what she had heard, geishas were experts at easing the tensions of a high-tech life-style.

Every week also saw a dinner-party or two for Western or Japanese friends, occasions which Dot was expected to join in with. The guests were usually, but not always, people from work. As a concession to Dot's presence, he always included some younger people in the party. But she wasn't craving for companionship of her own age group; the people she really liked talking to were Calum's friends and colleagues, people who gave her some background about the man who was her reluctant employer.

His job was clearly important, and his colleagues viewed him with considerable respect. Dot, who didn't know a semiconductor from a semiquaver, couldn't grasp the exact nature of his job, but she had already gathered that he was a key figure in a billion-dollar industry, and that the microchips he designed for the electronics giant who employed him went into dozens of products from home computers to motor-car engines.

'Calum's mind,' a friend once told her, 'puts him in the jet age while most of his contemporaries are still tinkering with steam engines.'

The first time she gained a real idea of his stature, however, occurred a few weeks after her arrival, when he took her and Pearl into Tokyo to visit the office where he worked.

Pearl naturally took it for granted that Calum was a Very Important Father, but Dot found herself rather overawed by the visit.

The corporation's headquarters were located in vast twin glass and steel towers in Tokyo's Manhattan-like centre. One of the towers was given over to administration, the other containing the research and development facilities.

The scale of Calum's offices, high up in the latter building, with a stunning view over the city, indicated the importance of his work. Another pointer to his prestige within this massive company was the elaborate courtesy with which he, and by transference Dot and Pearl, were treated by the staff.

This visit had been well prepared for. As he showed them the ultra-modern Microprocessor Development section, their progress was accompanied not only by regimented bowing and smiling, but by endless gifts.

At every division there was a toy for Pearl, and a gift of flowers or silk for Dot.

At first embarrassed, and then stunned, Dot found herself eventually carrying as many cellophane-wrapped bouquets as a royal personage on a walkabout. Calum commanded the respect of a great many people. When they made it back to Calum's sanctum after an hour and a half, she had to pass the haul to Ryoko, his pretty young secretary, to put in water.

She stared out of the window at the sprawling city below. A helicopter was speeding by, two blocks away, and as she watched, it landed on a nearby building, disgorging a handful of black-suited businessmen.

She had been too bemused by the kindness, and the huge scale of the offices, to follow Calum's explanations very well.

'I still haven't got much of an idea of the work you do,' she confessed, turning to him. 'Just that you're turning everything in the electronics world upside-down!'

He gave her an ironic glance. 'I'll show you something that may give you some idea of how the world of computers has changed in the last decade.'

Leaving Pearl to play with her new toys under Ryoko's eye, he led Dot to the lift.

'We're in the process of replacing one of the corporation's mainframe computers,' he said, pressing the button for the basement. 'It's all very secret, but you won't understand enough to make much of an industrial spy for the opposition.'

The basement was a windowless, brightly lit maze of spotless corridors, its denizens white-suited figures padding busily between offices.

The door he led her to opened on to a massive room, literally filled from floor to ceiling with electronic machinery. A team of white-suited mechanics were disassembling complex-looking boxes from the elaborate metal framework. As they watched, a section the size of a washing machine was unbolted. It was lowered unceremoniously to the tiled floor, where a heap of similar devices was already strewn, looking to Dot like million-dollar scrap.

'That's destined for the scrap-metal merchants,' said Calum, echoing her thoughts.

'Isn't it any good any more?'

'It isn't worth more than the metal it's made out of, though there's a bit of gold in some of the circuits.'

Her grey eyes widened as she took in the vast machine. 'And is all this stuff useless?'

He winced. '"All this stuff", as you call it, is one computer. Or rather, was.' His dark blue eyes wandered around the room. 'You're witnessing the final indignities of a great machine.'

'*One* computer?'

Calum nodded. 'This is ETRON I. It cost the corporation some ten million dollars, fifteen years ago. ETRON I could do thousands of calculations every second, but it had several problems. One was that it kept going wrong, and needed a full-time service team of a dozen people to maintain it. Another was that it used more power than the rest of the two towers put together. In Japan, that's expensive. So's space, which ETRON I needed too much of.'

They walked over to where the technicians were dismantling the giant computer, their casual attitude towards the once-mighty machinery now striking Dot as almost sad.

Calum exchanged a rattle of Japanese with them, then turned to Dot.

'They say ETRON I will be completely dismantled in a week. This room will then be turned over to a research laboratory.' His eyes glinted. 'Now I'll show you ETRON I's successor, ETRON II.'

He led her down the corridor to another, far smaller room. The atmosphere here was quite different. Several people were working at screens on desks set around a central glass cubicle. Inside the cubicle was a machine the size of an office photocopier.

'*That's* not the new computer, is it?' Dot gasped.

Calum nodded. 'That's ETRON II.'

'But how can something this size replace that enormous machine we saw just now?'

Calum smiled. 'ETRON II is three times as fast as ETRON I, and can store nearly fifty times as much data. It also costs under a million dollars, one thirtieth of the price in real terms, and can be plugged into the same circuit as an electric typewriter.'

Dot stared at him in awe. 'And you helped design ETRON II?'

'Well, ETRON II uses some of the microchips I helped develop.' He sounded casual. 'No doubt in fifteen years' time, ETRON II will be replaced by something the size of a matchbox, designed by a child of Pearl's age. But by then, I hope, I'll have taken early retirement and will be soaking up the sun in the Bahamas.'

He took her arm and led her, suitably overwhelmed, back to the lift.

'And microchips are those little things you showed us upstairs?' she asked, as they sped upwards.

'Here.' He took her hand and placed something in her palm. 'A souvenir.'

Dot studied the tiny greenish square in her palm. In its way, it was as beautiful as the finest jewellery. Though the circuits on it were practically invisible to the naked eye, she had peered into the microscope upstairs, and had seen that the little flake of silicon bore circuits as complex and ordered as the map of a great city.

Genius miniaturised.

Barbara Hescott had told her that Calum was a brilliant man, and she now realised that Barbara had only been telling the truth.

The visit left her very thoughtful, and almost afraid of Calum, for the next couple of days. Not that appreciating Calum's brilliance made him any easier to live with.

Charming as his staff obviously found him, he continued to treat Dot with something less than indifference.

One thing was clear: that beneath his hard, ironic mask, Calum Hescott loved his daughter profoundly. Love, in a man like this, was a powerful emotion. To get on the wrong side of it was to invite destruction.

In the past, Calum had obviously suffered acutely from his separation from Pearl when Clara had taken the child. Any hint that Dot was coming between him and his daughter was met with a stinging rebuke.

She had to keep reminding herself to try to understand the way he felt, and not be hurt by the aggressive attitude he took towards her.

That he cared deeply for Pearl was unquestionable. It was a protective emotion, and one that made him acutely suspicious of any outside interference. Specifically, interference from Dot.

She was, accordingly, taken aback when he let drop some grudging praise about Pearl's improving table manners after dinner one night.

'Clara used to let her eat with her fingers. She thought it was amusing.' They were sitting by the fire again, Pearl having been put to bed. Calum was having one of his not-too-common evenings in. 'In fact,' he added acidly, 'Clara wasn't a great stickler for formalities of any kind.'

Pearl's mother was a subject he hardly ever referred to, except indirectly.

'Barbara has told me a little about your late wife,' Dot replied cautiously. 'It's none of my business, of course, but she suggested that Pearl's mother wasn't exactly... well, a model parent.'

He leaned on one elbow, hard blue eyes watching her. 'That's the understatement of the century.'

'How often did you see Pearl after the divorce?'

Calum's expression grew stony. 'As often as my ex-wife would let me. Which was practically never.' His glass was empty, and he rose fluidly to pour himself a second whisky. 'You don't know much about Pearl's mother, do you, Miss Poppins? Let me tell you a little. Pearl's mother was a bitch. Don't look so pious,' he said drily, coming to sit in front of her again, 'it's the plain unvarnished truth. She was beautiful, but a bitch, and I was insane to marry her—the insanity that comes with an absurd infatuation. Unfortunately, we'd had Pearl before I found out. When I decided to leave her, my lawyers promised me I'd get custody of Pearl. They were wrong. The judge didn't even hesitate, even after all the dirt had been dug up about our miserable apology for a marriage. I lost my child, and Clara's idea of revenge was to make damned sure I saw as little of Pearl as she could possibly manage from then on.'

'I'm sorry,' Dot said quietly.

'Clara wasn't fit to care for a child. Like you, she was a great believer in pills. Pills to make you happy, pills to make you sleep, pills to wake you up. She gave them to Pearl, too.'

'Oh, no...'

'Oh, yes,' he said grimly. 'Mainly tranquillisers, to make sure Pearl didn't disrupt her fun at the wrong moment. Clara was very keen on fun. The kid ended up in a clinic for two days once, when her mother got the dose wrong. But then you're probably more scientific about it than poor Clara was, aren't you?'

Dot sat frozen in horror. She had had no idea what evil memories she would invoke when she had decided to give Pearl that pill. There was nothing she could say in her own defence.

His eyes were cold as ice. 'I could do nothing about it. I had to stand by and watch, because if I'd tried to interfere, she'd have got a court order to keep me away from my child—that's the kind of mother Clara was. Well, those who live by the pill die by the pill. That's very quotable, isn't it? It's certainly how Clara died. She got her pills mixed up, and went for a late-night swim off her current boyfriend's yacht.'

'Barbara told me it was an accident,' gasped Dot.

'The post-mortem revealed that she'd taken enough different drugs to make her black out in the water.' Calum swung round, and tossed another log on to the fire. A shower of sparks glittered momentarily up the chimney. 'I'm sorry it had to end that way for Clara, but at least I've got my daughter back. And I don't intend to let anyone get between us again.'

'I'm not trying to get between you,' Dot said quietly. 'I'm here to help. And I promise you I'll never give Pearl so much as a cough-drop again without your permission.'

Calum rose without replying. 'I have some work to do,' he said, terminating the conversation, as far as he was concerned. He stared down at her broodingly. 'You'll never be comfortable wearing Western clothes in this house. Ask Hanako to lend you a kimono or an *obi*, and get her to show you how to wear them.' He studied the lines of her hips and thighs. 'You're tall, but I think you're slim enough to carry it off.'

With a nod, he left her.

Dot rose wearily to her feet, noting that he had advised her to borrow, not buy. No doubt he didn't plan her to stay here long enough to make buying a kimono worth while!

She was wondering, as she headed for her room, whether she would still be here a month from now.

CHAPTER FOUR

WELL, I've been here six weeks now, Dot was writing, almost exactly a month later, and I can assure you that your great-niece has taken to Japan like a duck to water.

She looked out of the window at the drifting snow that was turning the garden into an exquisite symphony of white.

Or rather, like a duck to ice. It's getting very cold, and it keeps snowing in a sort of delicate way, as though it doesn't really mean it. By the time you get here, however, I'm sure it will be positively Siberian! Hanako-san tells me that the winters here can be very hard.

But to get back to Pearl-san, who is currently helping Oba-san with today's *sukiyaki* lunch: honourable daughter of the household is one very happy little girl. She has picked up masses of Japanese, far more than I have done, and chatters away to the servants, or her little Japanese friends, like a *shogun's* daughter.

I really feel she's getting over her mother's death, as the nightmares have stopped, and she seems happy and loved all day long.

Her revered father, of course, spoils her rotten, as does everyone else in the household, except honourable Dorote-san, who has to play the part of Black Dragon in the pantomime. I have to be very strict about bedtimes and manners and eating

of greens, and suchlike matters, or else Pearl
would be allowed to get away with murder by her
adoring elders.

Dot put her pen down and sat back on her cushion.
Though she hadn't succeeded in prevailing on Calum to
give her any truly Western-style furniture—'It would be
like painting a moustache on the Mona Lisa'—her room
had been made a great deal more comfortable. The wide,
flat cushions now made sitting on the floor at least
bearable, and she was slowly getting used to maintaining
the Japanese on-the-knees, bottom-on-the-feet posture
which looked so pretty, and gave one such awful cramp.
She had also, as her lord and master had advised,
adopted Japanese clothes, at least from time to time,
finding the loose garments eminently suited to indoor
life. Outdoors, she still preferred skirts or trousers.
Today she was wearing a pale brown linen kimono
with a tiny pattern of flowers, and a wide black sash,
which Hanako had fastened for her at the back. It wasn't
the full regalia, by any means, but it was very
comfortable, and—she flattered herself—rather fetching.
She was writing at a low, lacquered desk, with a little
brazier burning in one corner, keeping a promise she
had made in London to Barbara Hescott to keep her in
touch with events at Chinsanzo.
She reached out and touched the pale pink chrysanthemums in the vase beside her. They were exquisite,
sweetly feminine in form, with a faint fragrance that she
could detect all over her room.
Her cool grey eyes were absent as she studied their
intricate form, so beloved of Japanese poets and painters.
An odd factor of her life here, those chrysanthemums.
They were always present.

Whatever indignities Calum subjected her to, no matter how coldly or rudely he treated her—and at times he had almost driven her to the point of packing up and going—he insisted that these flowers should appear in her room, fresh every couple of days.

She had only found out they were here by Calum's wish when she had questioned Hanako about their source.

'Calum-san say Dorote-san must have fresh flower in bedroom, every-every day,' she had been told. 'Always different colour.'

What perverted gallantry provoked that little touch? Or was it just part of his wish that everything be in correct fashion, down to the flowers in the governess's bedroom?

There were times when she would willingly have swapped a mountain of crinkly-petalled chrysanthemums for one polite word, or one day spent without a sardonic remark.

Her eyes dropped to the glinting green microchip he had given her. She kept it on her desk, next to the flowers. For a moment her thoughts drifted, her lips parting slightly.

Then, sighing, she picked up her pen, and addressed Barbara once more.

As regards Calum, I have to say that he's no more keen on my presence here than he was when I last wrote to you. If anything, in fact, he's worse. He's rude, cold, unfriendly, impolite, disdainful, discourteous, downright inhuman—I wish I had my Thesaurus here to look up some more words to describe your nephew. I know you say he's a brilliant man, but that doesn't stop him from being an utter pig!

She hesitated, wondering whether to scratch that out. But it was the way she felt, and in any case, she didn't need to hold herself back with Barbara.

She underlined pig twice, her full lips compressed.

>He appears to think that I'm a kind of parasite in his household, and he seldom loses an opportunity of rubbing that opinion in. Any way he can find of embarrassing me, or making me feel like a clumsy, big-footed *gaijin*, and he seizes it with gusto.

>He makes me so angry sometimes I could throw something at him! I half suspect that he's trying to get me so mad that I'll just pack up and go. If it wasn't for Pearl——

Dot paused, then decided to leave that sentence unfinished. Barbara would no doubt be able to imagine the rest.

>Anyway, she concluded, apart from Calum-san, I have grown to love Japan in the past six weeks. It's still very strange to me, but the scenery is so beautiful, especially the mountains all around, and the people are so exquisitely kind and polite, that I feel quite at home already. You were right when you said I'd like it here. Don't bother answering this letter, it's all complaints and steam; but I have to let off steam in some direction, and you're the one who deserves it most richly.

>Looking forward greatly to seeing you in January. Pearl sends her love. I am enclosing some drawings of *samurais* and dragons that she did for me. Much love, Dorothy.

She folded the letter and slipped it into an envelope. These periodical outbursts of feeling did her a lot of good, though they probably made Barbara's grey hairs stand on end in Highgate. Well, why should Barbara be under any illusions about what life was like for her here? She would see for herself soon enough, when she came to stay.

The kitchen was a scene of industrious female activity, Oba-san at the stove, Hanako chopping vegetables, and Pearl messily stirring sauce into a bowl of cold rice.

Dot put her letter into the waist of Hanako's kimono, where Hanako kept all important items, and asked her to post it when she next went shopping.

'*Waskari-mas-ka*, Dorote-san. Excuse, please. Calumsan say please to go to study when possible.'

'*Hai.*' Dot groaned mentally. What had she done now? Being ordered to Calum's study was inevitably a signal for some reproof or other.

She straightened Pearl's pinafore and made a vain effort to wipe soy sauce off her shirt. 'How *do* you get so dirty? Don't forget your lesson at twelve.'

'I won't,' Pearl promised.

'Are you looking forward to it?'

'Yes!'

They were making great progress with Pearl's alphabet, and she could already read 'CAT', 'DOG' and 'BAT'. Today they were going to move on to the dizzy realms of V for 'VAN' and W for 'WET'. Dot was working hard at this, knowing how much literacy would mean when Pearl got to her first school. It would give her a head-start that would serve her right through her education.

Dot checked her appearance in the mirror, and went, sighing, to meet her employer.

Calum's study was in a block of its own, bounded by the garden on three sides. So much of the walls were taken up by rectangular windows that you got the impression of sitting outside, with only a roof over your head. The snowy gardenscape was lovely, tempered by the fire that burned inside.

She slid the doors shut behind her and went over to where Calum was sitting at a wide, flat table, the computer glowing green in front of him.

'You wanted to see me?'

'Hmm.' He turned from his work to glance at her with those dark blue eyes. 'Sit down.'

She obeyed, sinking to his level. As usual, he was wearing Prussian blue, the colour emphasising his tan and the authoritative, masculine cast of his features. 'Where's Pearl?'

'Assisting Oba-san with the lunch.' Dot smiled. 'Put "assisting" in quotation marks!'

He didn't answer her smile. 'Just make sure she never touches those knives.'

'She doesn't.'

Calum was studying her with that brooding intensity that always made her want to start fidgeting with her hair and clothes. 'Whose kimono is that?' he asked.

'Mine. I've tried to wear Hanako's, but they're too small. I bought this in the village.'

'Is that where my money goes?' Lean fingers reached out to turn the lapel aside, revealing the lacy top of Dot's bra. 'You're not wearing it properly,' he commented.

Dot flushed, and twitched the material out of his fingers. 'I know I'm not. But I'm comfortable, and that's what counts. What did you want to see me about?'

'A couple of things. One is that I'm taking Pearl skiing after Christmas.'

'Skiing?'

'I normally take a break around Christmas and New Year. We're going to a place called Hakuba. It's a popular resort, in the Japanese Alps. Those things out there,' he added, nodding at the distant peaks, now capped with snow. 'The slopes should be fantastic this year, judging by this month. I feel like having Pearl to myself just for once. With no extraneous interference.'

Dot tried not to be hurt at the pointed way he said it.

'How long will you be away?' she asked.

'A fortnight. We'll leave the day after Christmas, spend New Year in the mountains, and come back in the second week of January.'

She watched Calum's muscular hands, reflecting that he was a very strong man who loved hard physical activity. 'You won't push her too hard or too far, will you?' she couldn't stop herself from asking anxiously. 'She's not five yet.'

'She's just at the right age to learn, without hurting herself when she takes a tumble. She may get a little cold and wet, but she won't suffer.'

Dot winced slightly. What a tough-guy like Calum meant by 'a little cold and wet' could prove fatal pneumonia to a little elf like Pearl. But she wisely kept her peace. 'OK, I've got that. What else?'

'I've been invited out on Friday night by some associates from the corporation. Important people.' He picked up a pencil, and began spinning it between his fingers, not looking at her. 'It'll be a traditional evening—a visit to a *fugu* restaurant, then a nightclub, ending up in a geisha house.'

'How nice for you,' Dot said primly.

'These people are keen to meet you, for some inscrutable reason. I don't think they get to meet very many Englishwomen. So you've been included in the invitation. Do you want to come?'

'No, thank you,' said Dot. 'Was that all?'

Calum's eyes glittered. 'What do you mean, "No, thank you"?'

'I mean what "No, thank you" always means,' she replied.

'May I ask why not?' he demanded, frowning at her.

'In the first place,' Dot replied promptly, 'I'm a governess, not a national exhibit for your inquisitive colleagues. In the second place, I think that's the most graceless invitation I've ever had. And in the third place, I scarcely think a geisha house is the kind of atmosphere I would enjoy. If it's all the same to you.'

He drummed a devil's tattoo on his desk for a moment. 'As usual, your misconceptions about Japan are luridly wrong,' he said acidly. 'A geisha house is a very refined place, and not remotely what you obviously imagine it is. And it's a great honour for a woman to be invited to one. These people will have arranged the evening well in advance, and will have made special arrangements for your amusement. It isn't something you can turn down without giving offence.'

'But you don't want me there?' Dot asked calmly.

Calum shrugged his big shoulders. 'What has that to do with it?'

'Not much, perhaps. But I'm not coming.'

'Oh, for heaven's sake,' he said impatiently. 'What must I do? Get on my knees and implore you to come?'

'You could have asked me in a way that didn't give offence,' Dot said coldly. His rudeness was scarcely tolerable. *For some inscrutable reason*, indeed! 'You'll have to convey my apologies to your friends. And now, if you'll excuse me, it's time for Pearl's reading lesson.'

She rose, and left him staring after her with angry blue eyes. She put up with enough from him without being turned into a curiosity for his friends' amusement!

The lesson went well, given added zip by her satisfaction at having for once delivered a snub to Calum. She held Pearl's forefinger, tracing the large letters in the book with the tip, letting the patterns sink into Pearl's memory, from where, very soon, she hoped they would re-emerge as writing.

As always, they finished with a story from one of the picture-books, a favourite treat. She was running through her stock of English books very rapidly, she pondered. Pearl's curiosity seemed insatiable, and her love of stories was intense. She must ask Barbara to be sure to bring a fresh stock of books when she came.

Lunch was served *en famille*, Oba-san and Hanako sharing the big table. The *sukiyaki* was actually cooked at the table, and eaten steaming hot with chopsticks, the art of which Dot had finally mastered, right up to fried egg level.

Though Pearl chattered joyfully to her father about her progress at reading, Calum's face remained impassive, and he barely glanced at Dot through the meal. He had obviously been taken aback by the worm turning, and was not very pleased about it either.

At the end of the meal, however, while Hanako busied herself with the bowls, and Oba-san poured green tea, he turned to her, his expression stiff.

'Dorothy, I apologise for my ungracious invitation this morning.'

She stared at him blankly, almost spilling her tea in surprise.

'I would very much like you to come with me on Friday evening,' he went on, with an effort. 'Please will you reconsider your refusal?'

Dumbfounded, the first thought that came into her head was that these associates must be very important indeed. It must have cost him a great deal to utter that cold apology to someone he despised and resented so much.

'Thank you very much,' she heard herself replying, in the same formal way. 'I would love to come.'

Calum gave her a more-than-slightly ironic thank-you, and got up from the table to go back to the Tokyo office.

Dot had long since realised that Calum had a special attachment to Japan that had nothing to do with the fact that he was being paid a monumental salary for being here. He would not have bought this house if that attachment hadn't existed.

He was a man of taste and culture, behind the grim exterior, and his love for Japanese art was evident all over the house. What he appeared to enjoy most was the spareness, the restraint, of Japanese design, whether it was the simplicity of a flower painting or the stark lines of a garden.

For her own part, she was most drawn to his beautiful collection of *bonsai* trees. Some of them were over a century old, yet they were all dwarfs, tiny and exquisite things that grew in shallow ceramic dishes. She had watched the gardener carefully pruning and tending the rare plants. Sometimes, when one was in flower, or at a particularly beautiful stage, it would be brought into the house for a week or two, and displayed on a table.

But, most of the time, she felt very much lost by Japanese culture. Most of her judgements and comments seemed to irritate Calum, though she hadn't guessed how much until a couple of days later, when she happened to pause in front of a beautiful wooden screen that partitioned off part of his study.

The black-lacquered wood had been decorated with vertical rows of Japanese calligraphy, and the elegance of the script caught her eye.

'Japanese is so ordinary when it's printed,' she commented, 'and so beautiful when it's handwritten.'

Calum gave her a brief look.

'That's the first remark I've heard you make about Japan that wasn't utterly banal,' he said drily.

'Oh.' Dot felt her cheeks tingling. 'Do I—do I make a lot of silly remarks?'

'Do you ever make any sensible ones?' he countered acidly. That kink in his nose could make him look quite satanic when he was in an ironic mood. He nodded at the screen. 'That was painted in the seventeenth century, in Kyoto. It's a very rare piece.'

Dot swallowed her humiliation to ask, 'What does the writing say?'

'They're *sutras*. Buddhist verses.'

'I thought they must be poetry of some kind.'

'Not far off,' he shrugged.

She glanced at an ink painting that hung on the wall opposite, portraying a beautiful girl in a silk kimono, standing at the edge of a road. 'That's exquisite too. Who is she?'

Calum's frown relaxed. 'The painting is called "The Muddy Road". The writing underneath tells the story of a famous Zen monk called Tanzan.'

'What does a Zen monk have to do with a pretty girl?' Dot wanted to know, going up to the painting.

'Apparently, Tanzan and a fellow monk, Ekido, were going on a journey, when they met this very beautiful girl, hesitating to cross the road, because it was so muddy. She didn't want to get her kimono wet.' Calum came to stand beside her, looking at the painting with dark eyes. 'Zen monks are forbidden to have anything to do with women, especially young and pretty ones. Nevertheless, Tanzan hoisted the girl up in his arms and carried her across the road, for which she was duly grateful. But Ekido was scandalised.'

Dot had turned her attention to Calum's face. 'What happened?' she prompted.

'Well, Ekido was so offended that he didn't speak to Tanzan all day, until they got to their lodging for the night, when he couldn't hold it in any longer. He demanded to know why Tanzan had touched the pretty girl, when it was strictly forbidden.'

'What did Tanzan say?'

'He'd forgotten all about it. He looked at Ekido in surprise, and said, "But I left the girl at the side of the road. Have you been carrying her all day?"'

Dot smiled. 'I like that story, though I don't quite understand it.'

'I like it too, though I understand it all too well,' Calum observed, his face returning to its usual saturnine expression. 'And now, if you don't mind, I have some designs to finish.'

As she walked down the corridor, however, Dot's mind wasn't on Japanese art. She was vowing to herself that if ever another banal remark should rise to her lips in Calum's presence, she would bite her tongue off.

Tamotsu Koshima leaned forward. 'The *fugu* fish is one of Japan's greatest delicacies,' he told Dot. 'And it is also one of the most interesting dishes of our whole Japanese cuisine.'

'Really?' she said brightly. Tamotsu, a thickset man spreading to a paunch, was obviously a keen gourmet. She had met him several times at Calum's house, though the others were strangers to her.

They had been sitting in the restaurant for over an hour now, without so much as a bread roll to eat, but devastation had been wrought among several stone bottles of *sake*, a liquor which Dot found frankly over-powering. Judging by the bustle in the kitchen, the fabled *fugu* was on its way.

'*Fugu* chefs must train for over two years,' Tamotsu was informing her. 'There are over thirty steps to pre-paring the fish, prescribed by law! And the aspiring *fugu* chef must learn every one by heart.'

'Really?' She had to find another word. 'Really?' and 'My goodness!' were perilously close to the banal re-marks she had forsworn. 'Why so long? And why does the law prescribe thirty steps for preparing *fugu*?'

There was a chuckle round the table, which was not shared by Calum. 'Calum will tell you,' Tamotsu Koshima promised, in his staccato way, '*after* you taste the fish!'

'I look forward to that,' she smiled, not getting the joke. She was just praying that it wouldn't be raw.

So far, the evening had been anything but exciting. She had not been very pleased to find that she was the only woman in a party of five noisy, boisterously good-humoured men. Japanese wives, even Tokyo wives, it seemed, were not included in business entertainments.

Not much fabled Japanese impassiveness on view tonight, she thought. The interrogation she had been subjected to by Tamotsu and his friends had been jovial, but relentless; they were as hungry for information about English womanhood as Pearl was for stories about damsels and dragons, and she suspected that they found her answers equally entertaining.

Calum, though sitting beside her, was just leaving her to sink or swim. He had been talking quietly in fluent Japanese to the eldest of the party, Hiroshi Takemura, introduced as a senior scientist in his division. Talking about work was evidently his chief preoccupation.

As she had suspected, her presence tonight was nothing more than entertainment, and he had shown her only the barest courtesy or attention since leaving home.

For a change, he was in a suit, and she had to admit he looked devastating in it. With his tanned skin and dark hair, he did not look out of place in a restaurant filled with Japanese; and yet he was the handsomest man present, somehow subtly becoming the focus of attention, even though he was the quietest of the party.

She herself, Dot mused, must look very unusual, with her pale skin and elegant red dress. Not that anyone, least of all Calum, had bothered to compliment her on her appearance.

She was starting to regret having given way to his invitation. Whatever this evening was costing their hosts, and Calum had warned her it would be costing them a bomb, if the nightclub and the geisha house turned out to be equally dull, she would almost certainly fall asleep, and disgrace her lord and master utterly.

'Aha!'

Tamotsu's shout of delight was the signal for jubilation as several plates were borne in by beaming waiters.

'What do you think?'

Dot stared at the dish that was set down in front of her. It was extraordinary.

The fish had been shredded into tiny, petal-shaped slices, transparently thin. The petals had been arranged into a wide, pearly chrysanthemum, the stamens and leaves made of brightly-coloured slivers of vegetable. It was an incredibly intricate dish; used as she was to the way the Japanese loved to present their food, this looked literally too good to eat, and she said so.

But she was being urged on all sides to try it, and evidently no one was going to start until she had done so. She met Calum's dry glance, picked up her chopsticks, determined not to show up the extensive training she had been through at Calum's hands, and lifted a sliver to her mouth.

Her first taste confirmed her worst fears. The fish was indeed raw. But as she chewed valiantly, she decided that it was certainly delicious, with a strange, very un-fishy taste.

'It's super,' she said enthusiastically, picking up a second piece. It was delicate, and silky-smooth. 'Absolutely delicious!'

Amid laughter and applause, everyone tucked into the meal.

'Now,' she said, turning to Calum, 'tell me about it. Why does it take two years to become a *fugu* chef?'

'Because,' Calum said calmly, '*fugu* happens to be the world's most poisonous fish. It contains a toxin that's three hundred times as deadly as cyanide.'

Amid more laughter, Dot felt her face freeze. 'Are you kidding me?' she asked.

'Not at all.' There was an ironic glint in the deep blue eyes. 'It requires great skill to prepare the fish without turning it into your client's last meal on earth. Eating *fugu* is the culinary equivalent of Russian roulette.'

Cold all over, Dot stared at Calum. 'Is this—is this safe, then?' she demanded, her skin prickling.

'Almost completely safe,' Tamotsu assured her, then collapsed in laughter.

'Practically nobody dies from eating *fugu* these days,' another of the men assured her, grinning. 'Maybe fifteen a year. Not more.'

'Fifteen a year!' gasped Dot.

'But when they *do* die,' someone else chimed in joyfully, 'it is painful but quick.'

A story followed, in mingled Japanese and English, about some famous person who had recently died of eating *fugu* liver. Mercifully, the gruesome details were lost in floods of Japanese and gales of laughter.

'Good heavens!' Dot looked helplessly from her plate to Calum. 'I think you must all be mad!'

'It really is safe,' Calum said gently. 'They're pulling your leg.'

'You mean it isn't deadly?'

'Only if it's prepared incompetently, which this isn't. And it's illegal to serve the liver.'

Certainly, everyone round the table was eating with relish, making enthusiastic comments about the flavour. But Dot's appetite had quite gone. She leaned over to Calum, her dark hair brushing his cheek.

'How much does a dish like this cost?' she whispered.

'Around a hundred pounds,' he replied quietly.

'Oh, no!'

'Can't you manage it?'

'I don't think so,' she whispered miserably. 'And I'm terrified!'

'I promise you that there's no danger. All the poisonous parts have been removed, and the flesh has been thoroughly cleaned.' He glanced at her face briefly, blue eyes assessing her mood. 'But don't eat it if you don't want to.'

'How can I refuse?' she hissed.

'Easy,' he shrugged. 'What does it matter what it cost? If you don't want it, don't eat it.'

'Are you serious?'

'Absolutely.'

Dot stared at him. He meant it. She had expected him to insist that she consume the dish on pain of excommunication. She couldn't believe that he was letting her off the hook for once.

'There is a Japanese verse,' Tamotsu cut in, waving his chopsticks at her, 'which says, fools eat the *fugu* fish;

fools refuse to eat it.' He grinned. 'You don't like the flavour?'

'I love it.' Mustering her inner courage, she plied her chopsticks. She wouldn't disgrace Calum in front of his friends. If she was going to die, just let it be quick! But she would need some Dutch courage.

'I think I'm going to need a glass of *sake*.'

There was a brief hush round the table, and Dot wondered uncomfortably whether she had breached yet another ramification of Japanese etiquette. Calum leaned over to murmur in her ear again, 'Don't say the word *sake*. Or if you must, say *o-sake*.'

'Why?' she muttered.

'It's less shocking to Japanese sensibilities.'

She gave him a dry look. 'We all might die in agony, and you're worried about my saying *sake*?' She cleared her throat. 'Could I have a glass of *o-sake*, please?' she said aloud.

There were beams of approval as the drink was poured.

At least it was a delicious way to go. She concentrated on enjoying the food, even through Tamotsu's ill-timed and graphic description of the paralysis and convulsions that were the end of the unlucky *fugu* eater. The Japanese, she reflected, were a very strange people. Running through so much of their culture was a delight in dicing with death. It certainly added a piquant flavour to life—and to the smooth flesh of the *fugu*.

The *sake* undeniably helped it down. The alcohol came in tiny little eggcups, containing no more than a mouthful, but once she had had a few mouthfuls pressed on her, the amusing side of the evening began coming to the fore.

She finished her *fugu* triumphantly; not that Calum looked as though he cared one way or another. But at least she hadn't offended his friends.

Her valiant efforts with the *sake* and the *fugu* had earned her the respect of the party, and she was toasted as a fine example of her species, to which she replied in kind.

'Go easy on that stuff.' Calum's deep voice was soft in her ear. 'It's potent, and it'll lay you lower than the *fugu* if you're not careful.'

'This is my last,' she vowed, and coughed her way through a final eggcupful. 'Am I letting the side down?'

'Not so far.'

But it didn't escape her attention that he ordered her fruit juice from then on.

It was ten-thirty before they moved on to the bright lights of downtown Tokyo, by now a very festive party indeed. The nightclub, simply called Wow!, was thoroughly Western in style, with driving music being provided by a very slick live group on stage. Flashing strobes and whirling colours made a pulse-quickeningly effective lightshow, and when Calum took her hand and led her on to the crowded dance floor, Dot was ready to have some fun.

He danced well, using his strong arms and wide shoulders to protect her from the worst of the jostling. Like almost everywhere she had been in Japan, it was crowded to capacity. She was just starting to realise what a privileged life-style Calum led; in a country chronically short of space and privacy, the big house and extensive garden in Chinsanzo were signs of success indeed. She spun round in front of him, then sought refuge in his arms, laughing.

'What a crowd!' She had to yell at him over the crashing pulse of the band. 'I haven't died yet! Does that mean I'm going to be all right?'

'More or less,' he shouted back, and she caught the wicked glint of his white teeth.

'What's so funny? Why "more or less"?'

'I'll tell you later. Can you rock 'n' roll?'

'I'll try!'

The band had launched into a medley of fast Elvis numbers, evidently a favourite set, for the crowd were rock 'n' rolling joyously. Dot launched into the steps she knew, her hair tumbling around her face. Calum made her feel so secure. With implicit trust in his strength, she let him spin her round like a top, his fingers locked round her wrists. Unlike her own improvised movements, he was really expert.

'Do you come here often?' she laughed breathlessly. 'You're very good!'

'I'm almost old enough to remember this when it was new,' he grinned back. His hands cupped her slim, taut waist, and with a gasp, Dot felt herself surged into the air, so high that she was looking down on the upturned faces of other dancers. Then he let her down, keeping hold of one of her hands, so they could jive. She tried to follow the elegant manoeuvres of his lean legs, but he was far too quick for her, and he started laughing helplessly at her confusion.

Dim memories of having once been taught how to twist came back to her, and she switched to that, instead, which was far more of a success.

Breathless by the end of the medley, she was glad to slip into his arms for a slow number, and cool down a little against him. 'I didn't realise you were such a raver,' she panted.

'You're not so bad yourself,' he replied. Her dress was strapless, and his hand was warm on the bare skin of her back, not caressing, just holding her protectively. Whenever their bodies touched, she was aware of his hardness. He was a man who was taut with muscle wherever she touched him, yet his body had none of the heaviness of a dedicated weight-lifter. He was supple and light, a splendid male animal, like a stallion or a stag.

'You did well with the *fugu*,' he said, his mouth close to her ear. 'And your table manners are almost civilised. You only dropped one piece of fish down your front.'

'I thought you hadn't noticed!'

'I notice everything,' he smiled.

They danced among the surging crowds for an hour, Dot losing herself in the apparently endless variations of the light show, and the pleasure of being with a man who danced so well, and made her feel so feminine. She was seeing another side to Calum Hescott tonight, she reflected. She would never have believed that the grim-faced Calum, who could flay her alive with a few well-chosen taunts, could be such fun on the dance floor.

For almost the first time since meeting him, she felt happy in his company. It was ages since she had been out dancing with a truly exciting male, and Calum was little short of sensational. No matter what antagonism had passed between them, she could forget it tonight, as she indulged in the sheer sensual pleasure of being with someone who fitted in so well with her ideal of manhood—tall, strong, graceful, handsome.

They didn't talk much; what communication there was passed between their bodies, in the rhythm and touch of dancing.

It went all too quickly, and when at last he reminded her that they were neglecting their hosts, Dot was reluctant to leave the dance floor.

One of the younger men hustled her back on to it within five minutes, but it was not the same. He had nothing like Calum's presence, and in any case, Dot was starting to tire a little by now. Aware that she was feeling definitely flat out of Calum's company, she did her best to sparkle for the young Japanese.

But she caught herself glancing at her watch, and wishing she were sitting beside Calum instead. It was heading towards midnight, and there was still the mysterious pleasures of the geisha-house to come.

And if that was anything like other Japanese delights she had sampled so far, it would be more like an ordeal than a pleasure for the uninitiated foreigner!

'It's nearly three o'clock in the morning,' Dot yawned as the red Porsche finally purred up the garden drive at Chinsanzo. It had snowed again while they had been out, and the lights in the garden turned the white-trimmed trees into crystalline perfection. 'I've got out of the way of staying up late.'

'Staying up late?' Calum repeated drily. 'You were asleep for the last two hours.'

'I was not,' she defended herself. 'I was just lost in the beauties of the Song of the Cherry-Blossom Wind. All seventy-three verses of it.'

'Well,' he reminded her, 'I did warn you it wasn't going to be what you expected.'

'It certainly wasn't!' Dot couldn't help smiling as she thought back over the evening, recalling the difference between her highly-coloured expectations and the reality.

The geisha party had been a cross between excruciating culture and childish boisterousness. The geishas themselves, especially the formidable Mama-san, had behaved like good-humoured but firm nannies, supervising the entertainments, which had ranged from children's party games to extended recitals of poetry, with overpowering propriety.

They had, without exception, been middle-aged, highly painted, and as elaborately wrapped in their *obis* and regalia as rather aged and delicate Christmas presents from some Japanese Harrods.

Among the guests, there had been a great deal of laughter, dancing, crawling around the floor, and drinking.

Above all, drinking.

'I've never seen anyone drink the way those men did,' Dot said, as they let themselves into the silent house. 'And you didn't do so badly either.'

'That's what a geisha evening is,' said Calum. 'A children's romp with *sake*. Anyway, you had your share.'

'At least I didn't collapse, like Tamotsu-san.' They had left him more or less paralytic, in the chaste arms of Mama-san. One of her duties, apparently, was to make sure over-indulgent guests got home safely. 'Well, it was an education. And fun at times,' she smiled. 'Though I have to admit the cultural side was a little beyond me.'

'It was a long way beyond me,' he admitted. 'I dread geisha evenings, yet it's such a compliment to be asked to one.'

He switched the garden lights off, leaving the house in soft darkness.

As if by mutual consent, they went quietly to Pearl's door and peeped in. She was fast asleep with her rag doll. Dot tiptoed inside to tuck her in a little more cosily, then shut the door silently.

Calum was tugging his tie loose, revealing a tanned and muscular throat. 'I'm going to have a bath,' he said. 'I need to de-toxify all that *sake*. Are you coming?'

Dot paused in anguish. She suddenly didn't want the evening to end. Apart from that brief hour on the dance floor, she had hardly spoken to him all night, and she was intrigued to explore this rare, less hostile Calum. But she hadn't ventured into the bath since her first day here, and she certainly didn't think it was wise to do so now. On the other hand ...

'Ah, so sorry. In view of honourable female sensitivities,' he said with patient irony, 'we can leave the lights off. Honourable darkness will cloak revered female cherry-blossoms and peach-flowers from rude east wind of male eyes.'

He had mimicked the sing-song of Mama-san so wickedly that Dot was giggling helplessly.

'And if you don't get yourself excited,' he added, in his normal voice, 'you'll find it very beneficial after excessive examination of honourable *sake* bottle.'

'All right,' she decided at last. 'Might as well end the evening on a thoroughly Japanese note.'

Calum was already walking away. 'See you there—or rather, won't see you there.'

CHAPTER FIVE

THE bath-house, as Calum had promised, was in total darkness when Dot slipped in a few minutes later, wearing her robe and carrying a towel. As always, it was tropically warm and humid inside, and ghostly with steam. Calum was already in the water, but the most he could see of her was her brief silhouette against the snow-bright window, as she slid off her robe and padded gingerly down the stairs.

'Oosh!' she exclaimed.

'Take it slowly,' his deep voice advised. 'Go to the far end—it's much cooler there.'

'You didn't tell me that last time!'

'Didn't I?'

'No, because you were intent on boiling me alive,' she retorted, with a touch of bitterness.

It was definitely more tolerable where he had indicated. The pool had obviously been designed to provide a range of temperatures, and she found herself a spot where it was no hotter than a normal bath, and squatted luxuriously among the wraiths of steam.

'This really is a luxury,' she sighed, feeling herself instantly start to unwind. 'It must have cost you a fortune to have this thing built.'

'It did. But it was worth it.' As her eyes grew accustomed to the dark, she could just see that Calum was trickling water over his shoulders with the bamboo ladle. The gesture brought back a flood of memories of the last time she had been in here with Calum. His outline was classically male, wide shoulders tapering to a slim waist. 'Have you enjoyed the evening?' he asked casually.

'Yes, very much.'

'Despite the *fugu*?'

'I even enjoyed the *fugu*,' she smiled, smoothing her arms with her hands under water, 'though I'm glad to be still alive.' She frowned. 'It's tasty, but not exactly ambrosia of the gods. Why on earth do they risk their lives to gobble such a poisonous little delicacy?'

'The answer, if there is one, is very complicated.' There was a hint of amusement in the deep voice. 'But one of the reasons is that *fugu* is supposed to be wildly aphrodisiacal.'

'No! Is it?' said Dot, taken aback.

'So they say. Especially for women. Judging from the portion you ate, you ought to turn into an insatiable nymphomaniac some time tonight.'

'Or a candidate for honourable cemetery,' she shuddered.

'I'd definitely prefer the former,' Calum smiled.

'There isn't any truth in that, surely?' Dot pressed, feeling uncomfortable at the line the discussion had taken, but fascinated none the less.

'Who knows?' he replied, with the same husky amusement in his voice. 'Let's sit here and find out.'

She paddled to a cooler shoal in silence. 'There's no such thing as an aphrodisiac, anyway,' she said primly. 'It's all nonsense.'

'There speaks rational Western woman,' Calum said calmly.

'Well, *fugu* certainly can't be an aphrodisiac!'

'It can't be deadly poisonous either, I suppose?' With a ripple, he slid into the water up to his neck, and drifted towards her. 'I hope you're thoroughly ashamed of your misconceptions about geishas, anyway.'

'Oh, I am. I used to have such lurid imaginings about what you got up to when you went out to a geisha house. Or should I say o-geisha?'

'Not with me, at any rate. What sort of imaginings?'

'Well, dissipated orgies, I suppose. Wild sex and so forth.'

He seemed amused. 'And you were disappointed by the truth?'

'Rather. They were so old! I'd expected seductive young things in transparent outfits, and all sorts of hanky-panky going on behind pornographic silk screens.'

'You were about the most seductive young thing there. A true geisha is only considered really fully trained when she's in middle age. And the emphasis is on composing music and poetry to a high level, and providing intellectual entertainment for her customers.'

'How odd.' The light glistened on his wet shoulders as he ran his fingers through his hair. Dot watched his dark silhouette. 'Then all that stuff you hear about geishas is false?'

'Not exactly. There are geishas who specialise in satisfying the more physical needs of their clients.'

'I hope they're younger than the ones we saw tonight!'

'Oh, yes. They're both young and beautiful. They have less to learn, you see. Instead of learning how to compose *tankas* and *haikus*, and play the *samisen*, they become experts in the arts of the bedchamber.'

Dot glanced down at the paler shadow of her body in the dark water. 'Have you—have you ever been to one of those?' she asked, colouring as she did so. The *sake* had loosened her tongue dangerously.

Calum laughed softly. 'Now what makes you ask such a very personal question?'

'Just honourable thirst for knowledge. You sound as though you know what you're talking about.'

Devastatingly handsome though he was, Dot knew that there was no permanent woman in Calum's life. Though he had no shortage of female acquaintances, there wasn't a girlfriend or a lover, as far as she could tell. She had long since guessed that his sexual liaisons must be casual, and this was a provocative lead to follow.

'Would you be shocked if I said yes?' he asked.

'I think I'd be more disappointed if you said no,' she smiled. 'I may be a governess, but I'm not a prude, Calum. After a disastrous marriage like the one you went through with Clara, you'd be a fool to think of anything remotely permanent just yet.'

'Exactly,' he said calmly. 'Except I would delete the "just yet" and substitute "ever again".'

'You don't like women, do you?' she challenged him.

'On the contrary, I adore women,' he retorted.

'Not as people,' she decided. 'You're far too ironic and cynical to really be fond of women as people.'

Calum's laughter was husky. 'Now what makes you say a thing like that?'

'Experience,' she replied meaningfully.

'Oh, yes,' he said casually, 'I forgot. I'm an utter pig, underlined twice. Any way I can find of embarrassing you, and I seize it with gusto. And I make you so angry sometimes you could throw something at me.'

Dot gasped in horror, recognising the intemperate words of her letter to Barbara.

'How did you get hold of my letter?' she demanded, wide-eyed.

'Hanako brought it to me. She seems to think it's a point of loyalty to bring me all your letters.'

Dot was speechless for a moment. 'But—but that's *iniquitous*!' She was thinking, with tingling cheeks, of other things she had written about Calum in her letters, none of them complimentary. 'How *dare* you read my mail?'

'I don't do it as a regular thing. Your correspondence,' he said drily, 'isn't exactly riveting. But you hadn't sealed that particular envelope properly, and— well...' his dark shape shrugged indifferently, 'call it honourable thirst for knowledge.'

'Call it dishonourable prying!' snapped Dot. 'Well, at least you didn't read anything good about yourself, for which I'm sincerely thankful!'

'Oh, I'm not so sure. If my aim was to get you so mad that you'll pack up and go, as you said in that letter, then I might have been pleased to see how well I was getting under your skin.'

She glared at him in tight silence. 'Well,' she said at last, 'can you deny that that's exactly what your aim is?'

'I didn't want a governess for Pearl in the first place,' he said calmly. 'You know that. But to say that I'm waging some kind of campaign against you is plain hysterical.'

'Come on! Are you saying you wouldn't rejoice if I announced that I was leaving tomorrow?'

'Personally,' he replied in the same indifferent tone, 'I wouldn't shed any tears. But my daughter clearly adores you. If it wasn't for Pearl——'

'If it wasn't for Pearl——' she echoed grimly.

There was a silence, broken only by the trickle of the waterfall behind them.

'Well,' Dot said stiffly at last, 'you're certainly full of surprises, Calum-san.'

'I don't think so,' he contradicted her. 'I certainly haven't tried to disguise my feelings about your presence here.'

'You did a pretty good job tonight,' she retorted, thinking about that blissful hour in the nightclub.

'What do you mean?'

'Oh, nothing,' she said wearily. 'Forget I spoke.'

'But I'm interested,' he said quietly, moving to her. 'You think I treated you in some special way tonight, and I want to know how.'

'Just like a human being for once,' she said bitterly. 'Or, better, almost like a woman.'

'Don't I treat you like a woman?'

'You've read my mail,' she snapped, 'so you know how I feel.'

'And that's the way I truly appear to you? A tyrant? A pig, underlined twice?'

'Can you ever recall having said one kind thing to me?' Dot countered bitingly. 'Can you remind me of one thing you've ever said to me that wasn't cutting, humiliating, or belittling?'

'Yes. I once told you you had beautiful eyes. Is that the kind of thing you want me to say?'

'Of course not,' she said in confusion. 'I don't want empty compliments, Calum.'

'But it wasn't an empty compliment,' Calum replied softly. 'Your eyes are truly remarkably beautiful. The look in them is defiant, and yet gentle. It taunts, and yet it caresses. Sometimes they have the look of a virgin, or a doe, or some gentle creature that hardly knows the world. At other times they flash, like grey fire. How do so many lovely things live in your eyes, Dorote-san?'

'I don't think this is——' Dizzily, she groped for words.

'And that mouth.' As though he could see in the dark, like a leopard, he reached out to touch the satiny skin of her lower lip. 'Cool, touch-me-not, slightly arrogant. Yet so soft, so enticing...'

Dot was suddenly acutely aware of their nakedness. Dark as it was, his words were making her flush hotly, as though her skin were illuminated to his gaze.

'You've had too much *o-sake*,' she said brusquely. 'I'm getting out, and going to bed.'

'As you please,' he replied, a harsh edge to his voice.

They both waded over to the steps, Dot emerging first, and moving over to her towel. She picked it up, and pressed it to her burning face. Damn him! Damn his cutting words and his male arrogance! She had been a fool to ever open herself up to him. Nobody but a fool exposed tender flesh to sharkskin.

She wasn't aware that he had come up behind her until she felt his hands close around her shoulders, and his mouth brush the back of her neck.

'Is there some truth in that *fugu* legend?' he murmured, in a husky voice that made her skin suddenly shudder into gooseflesh. 'Or is it just you?'

'I told you,' she said, trying to sound brisk, 'there are no such things as aphrodisiacs.'

'Then it must be you.' He turned her to face him, lean fingers reaching to touch her hair. 'You were beautiful tonight, Dorothy.'

'How do you know? You didn't look at me above three times!'

'I looked at you as much as was wise,' he replied. 'Or I might not have been able to tear my eyes away again.' His fingers were caressing her throat, her lips, studying her face by feel, in the darkness. His touch was sure, gentle, an intoxication that made her melt.

'What are you doing?' she whispered.

'Seeing you—with my fingertips.' She registered, as if far away, that he was caressing her cheek, his fingers trailing round her chin to cup it, and draw her face forward to his.

Her eyes, as though drugged, closed helplessly. She felt his lips touch hers, warm and firm. She tried to push him away, but the supple, hard flesh under her palm was stronger than her will. There was a thudding in her ears as she felt his arms draw her close, his mouth gently forcing hers open. She felt dizzy, remote from what was happening.

I want and do not want. Dot looked up blindly into his face, the face she could not see, and yet which she knew so well. So handsome, so potently male, the smoky expression in his eyes both terrifying and yet paganly exciting.

She reached up to touch his cheek, feeling the harsh stubble of his beard, tracing the crooked line of his nose to reach the outline of that devastating mouth.

She could feel his naked body touch hers, the lean strength of his thighs against hers, the mystery of his loins.

'No,' she gasped against his possessing lips, 'no, stop, please——'

Calum whispered her name, his mouth roaming over her face. Her arms were sliding around his neck, for support, not because she was consenting to what was happening. The movement brought his hard chest against the taut peaks of her breasts, sending an electric thrill through her.

His hands slid possessively down her flanks, cupping the swell of her hips and pulling her against him, holding her there with one hand in the small of her back when she tried to writhe away at the contact with his hard, thrusting manhood. With his other hand he gently traced the curve of her breast, finding the unbearably tight peak, giving it the release of a rough caress.

'I want you,' he said harshly, his throat tight with passion. 'You've been a thorn in my side...why shouldn't I pick the rose?'

'Calum...' She was responding to him without thought or volition, her fingers feverishly caressing the wet tousle of his dark hair, her spine arching like a bow under his strong hands.

Mingling with the hot desire, the raw excitement that was making her blood race like champagne, were the frail ghosts of her more sensible feelings. What did he take her for? Some kind of available handmaiden who was here for his pleasure?

She was insane to permit this, to let him do this to her.

Yet you want him, an inner voice hissed in her ears, you want to be his, even though he despises you, and if you can't have his respect, you'll settle for what you can get...

She cried out huskily as he kissed her nipples, stars of desire that thrust hard and jutting against his mouth. Her arms cradled his head against the neat, taut curves of her breasts, her stomach shuddering. He sank down before her, his arms encircling her hips as he kissed the flat, smooth plane of her belly, her slender thighs, the downy skin of her loins.

Dot shrank away, aching with desire, then knelt with him, her mouth seeking his.

The sum total of her experiences with men had been flirtations and cuddling, the sort of intimacy that had finite limits, and finite ends.

This was different. This naked, shuddering contact was frightening in its intensity, the pleasure it gave like the rush of some fierce drug in the bloodstream.

But this too would stop. It too was a game, a flirtation that was just more potent and more exciting than any flirtation had been before. It would go a little too far, and then it would come to an end, when she sat up, brushed back her hair, and announced cheerfully that it was time for coffee.

Wouldn't it?

Calum's naked body was firm and lean under her seeking palms, the hard curves of well-developed muscles responding like liquid bronze to her touch. As their mouths quested, his fingers trailed down her ribs, across her stomach, making Dot gasp with desire. He responded with a groan, a deep sound that whipped her senses.

'So you detest me?' he whispered harshly. 'So I'm the rudest man you've ever met?'

He was caressing the silky skin of her inner thigh, erotic circles that moved upwards with maddening slowness, until...

'No,' she whimpered, arching at the intense sweetness of his touch. 'No, Calum, stop...'

She could pretend it was a game, up till now, could pretend that it would all end just when she wanted it to, leaving her with those delicious, unsatisfied feelings that were both pleasant and painful.

Not any more. The force in her was growing too strong for her to control. This had only one end, and that was their making love, here on the warm stone floor. As he caressed the melting essence of her womanhood, waves of intense pleasure surged through her, making her gasp and press her face to his muscular chest as she clung to him. His touch was expert, sinfully intense, a delicate and maddening rhythm that she suddenly couldn't bear any longer.

'No!' She squirmed away from him and got to her shaky legs. She groped in the dark for her gown and pulled it over her nakedness.

She had been insane!

Hadn't he just told her that he would never think of a permanent relationship with a woman again? That he wouldn't care if she left Chinsanzo tomorrow?

And knowing all that, she had been on the verge of letting him take her virginity, about the only thing that really meant something to her!

'What's wrong?' he asked, getting to his feet, and coming over to her.

'Nothing's wrong,' said Dot in a trembling voice. 'I'm going to bed, Calum.'

'Silly girl. Come back here!' His fingers sought her wrist, but she jerked herself free.

The violence of her movement told him she wasn't fooling. His voice became grim. 'What kind of game is this?'

'It was never a game, Calum. I'm just not here for your pleasure, that's all.'

'My pleasure?' His tone was biting. 'Are you telling me you weren't enjoying it?'

'I'm telling you that I don't want to continue. And you were very wrong to start it.'

'Is everything wrong that you don't understand? What are you so uptight about?'

'You despise me. I'm nothing to you.' Her voice was low and unsteady, echoing the way her whole being was aching. 'And yet you want to make love to me. Can't you understand that I might not want to be just an available female body in the darkness?'

'We'll put the lights on, then,' he retorted. 'Sex has nothing to do with our personal feelings. This is the twentieth century, Dorothy.' His wet skin gleamed in the dark as he reached for her. 'Don't be a fool. I'm dying for you!'

'Then you'll just have to die,' she said, turning away. 'Sex happens to have a great deal to do with *my* personal feelings.'

'You little prig! If you don't want to make love, then that's your privilege. Just for heaven's sake don't be so bloody moral about it!'

His tone reminded her so sharply of similar situations with Jack Taunton that she felt pain lance through her. 'It isn't a question of morality,' she said in a low voice. 'I'm just not here for your convenience.'

'Then you shouldn't have gone half-way. That was despicable.'

The word stung like a slap. 'You started, not me. You shouldn't have eaten so much *fugu*, if that's what it does to you.'

'I could——' His voice shook with anger. 'Damn you, Dorothy,' he said grimly. The snowy light from the window glittered coldly in his eyes. 'I'll make you pay for this!'

'I have no doubt you will,' she replied tightly. 'For all your complaints about how much I'm costing you, you're very good at making me pay. It seems to me I've been paying from the moment I got here.'

She walked out, across the covered courtyard, and back into the house. She was crying quietly as she shut her flimsy bedroom doors and crept between the sheets.

What a horrible, painful end to an evening that had been so sweet!

Calum had behaved like—like an animal. She had a hot remembrance of his arousal, hard and aggressive against her skin, and twisted round with a little gasp, her loins tightening with aching desire.

And she? How had she herself behaved?

Had that really been herself, squirming and writhing in Calum's arms like a cat on heat? Self-disgust was bitter

in her mouth. She had been betrayed. She had been lured
into a compromising situation by a ruthless seducer, and
that was her only excuse. For the rest, she had behaved
with disastrous lack of professional ethics. The blow to
her self-esteem was a severe one.

Did tonight mean that her time here was over? Would
he dismiss her first thing tomorrow? Or should she leave
of her own accord, and use the other half of her return
ticket to London? Let Barbara find another governess,
a woman either willing to play geisha to her employer,
or a witch too old to interest him.

She pressed her wet face against the pillows. Silly. Silly,
silly. She mustn't think such weak thoughts. She was
overwrought, overtired, and had certainly drunk too
much *sake*. There was no possibility of leaving. What
about Pearl? She couldn't just abandon her charge,
whatever had happened between Calum and herself.

Tomorrow all this would be a dream that had passed
in the night, and they would both start to forget that it
had ever happened.

Except that she knew she would never forget tonight.

In the pastel-shaded book of her experiences, this was
a glaring red page that told her one thing, and one thing
alone.

That, despise her though he might, she was starting
to become far more deeply involved with Calum Hescott
than was good for her.

'But *why* can't Dot come?'

Dot's sinking heart plummeted another notch. 'Because Dot has all sorts of things to do at home,' she told
Pearl. 'I haven't got the time to come skiing with you!'

But Pearl knew an evasion when she heard one. And
she also knew where the real decision-making authority
lay in this matter.

'Why can't she come?' she demanded from Calum, her big blue eyes searching his face.

He hoisted her up in his arms. 'Because she doesn't *want* to come,' he said firmly. 'She's just said so.'

'She does want to come! She told me she'd miss me. And I'll miss her! Who'll read my story at night?'

'I'll read your story,' Calum assured her patiently. His eyes met Dot's, and they were icy-cold. Naturally he would suspect she had something to do with the child's behaviour tonight.

As if anything was needed to worsen relations between her and Calum right now!

Since the night they had gone out, he had barely spoken to her once. His attitude towards her had produced a frost in the air that had affected the whole household. Oba-san and Hanako were fully aware of it. For a fortnight they had moved around the house silently, with downcast eyes, like mice afraid of waking a sleeping giant. Now, as they cleared the table after dinner, they wore the mask-like faces of *kabuki* actors, as if determined not to notice the storm-clouds that were brewing ominously overhead.

Pearl, with a child's instinct, had known something was wrong over the past week or two. Dot could sense the uneasiness in her. But Pearl had kept it all inside until the announcement that her beloved Dot was not coming on the skiing trip to Hakuba after Christmas.

And now, disastrously, the pent-up tensions were coming out.

'But *I* want her to come! I'm not going if Dot isn't coming!'

'Don't be silly, sweetheart.' Calum's dark brows were coming down. 'Everything's been arranged by now, and it can't be changed, even if I wanted to.'

'I'm not going if Dot isn't coming!'

'Yes, you are,' he contradicted her. 'It'll be lovely, with all the snow.'

Pearl's voice rose sharply. 'It won't!'

Dot bit her lip. Pearl hadn't thrown a single tantrum, not a real one, since leaving England, and Dot had prayed that they were becoming a thing of the past. But the hectic colour in the little girl's cheeks was an ominous sign.

It occurred to her that Calum had never seen one of Pearl's tantrums. If she chose to throw one now, it would be something of a shock to him. And Dot herself, as being the 'cause' of it, could expect another wave of anger directed at her.

Calum was attempting to humour the child, but Pearl's passion was too deep to yield to the tickling games she normally loved, because 'I won't', and 'I don't want to', were the rebellious refrains she recurred to. And when Calum tried to tell her about the fun she was going to have on the ski slopes, a few foreboding tears started crawling down her plump cheeks.

It was time to intervene, before one or the other of them lost their tempers—and they both had Hescott temper a-plenty to lose!

Dot folded her kimono round her hips and rose to take Pearl from Calum's arms.

'It's time for your bath,' she said firmly. 'Say goodnight to Daddy, and let's go and get your rubber duckies.'

'I don't want my bath!'

'Yes, you jolly well do.' Dot bore her away, wearing her I'm-not-having-any-nonsense face, which almost always worked.

Bathtime was normally fun for both of them, but not tonight. Pearl protested mutinously all the way to the bath, and once in, was uncooperative and sulky. There were little hot smudges under her eyes that warned that the matter wasn't settled yet, just resting.

Dot could sense Pearl still simmering as they prepared for bedtime. In a sense, the child's reaction was understandable. She had lost a mother, and transferred so much of her affections to Dot that the prospect of a parting was naturally upsetting. To little Pearl, two weeks away from Dot would seem like two years.

But it was also a very awkward situation, given the strained relations between her father and her governess. The look Calum had given her as they had left the table had been grim.

Curled up in her bed, Pearl listened in silence to the fairy-tale Dot read her. The high colour gradually subsided from her cheeks, and towards the end of the story, her eyelids started to droop, much to Dot's relief.

As Dot stooped to kiss her, she peered up sleepily.

'I don't *want* to go to that place with Daddy. Not unless you come.'

'We'll see. Go to sleep, now.'

'"We'll see" means "no"!'

Dot smiled, and switched the bedside lamp off. She stared down at Pearl's face, watching it relax into sleep. She had grown so close to this little mite over the past autumn. Far closer than she ever had done with previous charges.

Intent on avoiding a confrontation with Calum, Dot headed straight for her own bedroom. Unluckily, though, Calum was talking on the hall telephone, and with a glitter in his deep blue eyes, he motioned her to wait.

He concluded his conversation with a Bren-gun rattle of Japanese, and put the receiver down. He took Dot's arm with ungentle fingers and propelled her back to the sitting-room.

'Now,' he began bitingly, sliding the door shut behind them, 'what the hell is this all about?'

'If you're talking about Pearl's little upset tonight, I don't think you need worry. She'll get used to the idea.'

'Oh, she will, will she?' He turned and walked to the drinks cabinet. In the black kimono he was formidable, an embroidered dragon spewing fire across his wide shoulderblades.

He poured two whiskies, and though Dot didn't want the glass he thrust at her, she deemed it wise to accept.

'Have you put the kid up to this?'

The abrupt question almost made her choke on the whisky.

'Of course not,' she said indignantly. 'What would I put her up to it for, in any case?'

'No doubt you have your own motives,' he replied grimly. 'Why is she so insistent about your coming?'

Dot hesitated, then shrugged. 'She's fond of me,' she said simply.

'Yes,' he agreed drily. 'You've seen to that.'

His tone was so cutting that her temper started to rise.

'I've given her a little love,' she retorted, 'which is hardly brainwashing.'

'You expect me to believe that tonight's performance was a bolt from the blue?'

'Of course I don't. The reasons for it have been staring you in the face, but they're not the reasons you imagine.'

'Oh?' He swirled the amber liquid in his glass, then tossed it down, his mouth twisting into a grimace. His eyes never left her face. 'What are the reasons, then?'

'You, for a start.'

Calum's dark good looks could sometimes be almost frightening. Whatever it did to his staff, that expression certainly awed her. He towered over her now, eyes narrowed into smoky slits. 'Me?' he repeated.

'Yes,' Dot nodded, standing her ground. 'And as for kicking up a storm, tonight was nothing to what I've seen her do in the past.'

'What are you talking about?'

'She used to throw tantrums whenever she couldn't get her own way. Quite a spectacular performance, I assure you.'

'Clara had her spoiled rotten,' he commented harshly.

'Well, I think it was more than just spoiling. Tantrums aren't always deliberate naughtiness. They sometimes happen when a child feels helpless, and its emotions get too much for it to bear.'

'And I'm the one giving Pearl all these emotions, am I?'

'Well, you know she's fond of me, and she certainly adores you. Pearl's not too young to understand that your behaviour towards me is cold and rude. Naturally, any sign of hostility between the people she loves upsets her.' She gulped at her own whisky to give herself courage. 'She's already been through a divorce, and the death of her mother. A wise father would try not to upset her any more than necessary.'

Calum actually snarled, like a panther. 'Are you telling me I have to start treating you like a wife, for Pearl's sake?'

'That's not necessary,' said Dot, her face flooding with colour. 'A little politeness, and not being quite so abrasive to me in front of her, would be quite adequate.'

His eyes considered her face with little pleasure. He was too intelligent not to see the force of what she was saying. But it was obviously not a palatable idea.

Dot felt a wave of ironic grief. Did he really, she wondered sadly, have to be coerced into treating her with kindness? She had never been in a situation where someone who was so important to her viewed her with such contempt.

How was it that she felt so much for him, and he so little for her?

'And now she's kicking up a storm because I want to have a fortnight off with her,' he said darkly.

'Well, perhaps she doesn't quite understand the attractions of winter sports yet,' Dot ventured. 'That doesn't mean she doesn't love you. You're the centre of her universe.'

He took the glass out of her fingers and went to pour them two more whiskies. 'If I were that important to her,' he growled, the dragon spitting fire at her from his broad back, 'she'd be eager to come to Hakuba, not crying her eyes out about it.'

'She just needs a little understanding.'

'Which you have in good measure,' he replied, giving her the refilled glass. He stared at her unwaveringly, passionate mouth compressed into a hard line. His gaze was so hard to meet that Dot looked away. 'This is exactly the kind of situation I didn't want to arise,' he said at last, his voice bleak. 'I knew it was a mistake to let you stay here. I knew you'd come between me and the child.'

'Oh, Calum, that isn't true——' Suddenly, it dawned on her like a flash of light. He was *jealous* of her closeness with Pearl!

Yes, it was there in his eyes. He resented her bond with Pearl. He had done for months past.

He had had his daughter taken away from him once, and he was prepared to fight like a tiger to stop the same thing ever happening again, whether it was logical or not.

Her perfectly shaped mouth had frozen open, but now she closed it. There really wasn't much she could say.

'"Why can't Dot come?"' he said bitterly, mimicking his daughter. 'Such an inane little name—*Dot*. It's like something out of a cartoon. How did you end up with a name like that?'

'I've always been called Dot,' she replied in a small voice. 'I know it's a silly name.'

'It's the only name I ever seem to hear Pearl saying. Maybe I should send you back now,' he said quietly, 'before it's too late.'

Dot stood motionless, knowing that her fate hung in the balance. Perhaps sending her away, she suddenly felt, would be the best thing for everyone concerned.

To be sent home, and never to see Pearl or Calum Hescott again, would be agonising. But it might save her, in the long run, from a far more damaging hurt. Staying on here, with a man who obviously detested and resented her, and who had such a power to wound her, was a certain recipe for a broken heart.

And she couldn't justify staying for Pearl's sake, when she was so obviously becoming a source of discord in the household.

'Now is the obvious time to do it,' Calum brooded, as though she wasn't there, as though her feelings meant nothing to him. 'You could leave while we were in Hakuba. Then you'd be gone by the time we got back. Pearl would have had a fortnight to forget you in, and at the end of the month, Barbara will be here to fill the gap. The break would be much easier.'

Dot stared down into her whisky, her heart thudding heavily against her ribs. She wanted to cry out, to implore him not to send her away, but she bit down the words with as much self-control as she could muster.

Then Calum turned abruptly away. 'I'll have to think about it. In any case, I don't intend to tolerate any nonsense from Pearl about this. Tomorrow we're going to fit her out with skis and skiing clothes—that'll take her mind off things. I'll impress upon her that she's coming, and that you're staying. That'll be an end of it.'

Dot fidgeted with the drink she didn't want, dangerously close to tears. 'Whatever you say.'

He was staring out of the window at the snowy twilight. 'It isn't really your fault,' he said in a cold voice. 'The idea was a bad one from the start. I should never have let Barbara talk me into it.'

'She was only thinking of Pearl.'

'You have no children,' he said tightly, 'so you can't understand.' He drained his glass, giving that same grimace, as thought he were using the whisky to dull some inner pain. 'Are your parents living?' he asked absently.

'No,' Dot replied. Her soft mouth trembled for an instant. 'They were—they were both killed when I was a child.'

'Ah,' he muttered under his breath. 'Barbara told me, but I'd forgotten. A car crash.' He turned to face her, drawing down his brows. 'How old were you?'

'Twelve. Just short of twelve.'

'Have you any brothers or sisters?'

'There was only me,' she said with an attempt at a smile. 'Just as well, really. It would have made things rather more difficult if there had been other children.'

'Rather more difficult,' Calum repeated drily. 'Who brought you up after your parents died?'

'I'm not sure,' she said, with an attempt at humour. 'There wasn't really anywhere for me. I went to boarding school in Yorkshire until O levels, and in holiday time I alternated between my grandmother and my father's sister.'

'That sounds like a hard road,' he commented.

'It had its ups and downs.'

Talking about it was upsetting her, as it sometimes did. She wanted to turn and flee, but Calum was still watching her in that dispassionate, hooded way.

'How did it happen?'

The accident itself was something Dot never talked about, and it was an effort even to give him the bare details. 'We were going to Scotland on holiday—I was to have my twelfth birthday there. A truck lost control coming the other way, and crossed the central reservation, right into our path.' Her mouth was dry. 'They were both—both killed instantly. I got away with concussion and some fractured ribs.'

Calum studied her narrowly. 'You sound very calm about it.'

'It was a long time ago.' How many times had she said that? *It was a long time ago.* Like an incantation, to stop the pain from catching her under the heart again.

'You describe it as though it were something you'd read about. Don't you have any personal memories of the accident?'

The terrible noise, the pain, the fear. The knowledge that something dreadful had happened, and that the world would never, ever be the same again.

'One or two details,' she said with an effort. 'But the knock on the head made it all pretty much of a blur. I was only conscious for a short while on the motorway.'

'It sounds as though you were lucky to survive.'

'I didn't think so at the time.' The pain was coming back, taking her breath away. She put her glass down, and unwittingly laid her hand over her aching heart. 'Do you mind if I go to bed now? I'm rather tired.'

'You're white,' Calum noticed, coming forward with a frown. He touched her cheek with warm fingers. 'And you've gone as cold as ice.' Realisation made his eyes widen. 'Does it upset you to talk about it?'

Dot's thick, dark lashes veiled the pain in her limpid grey eyes. 'A—a little,' she nodded, her voice uneven.

'Damn,' he said quietly, taking both her elbows and looking down into her face. 'Why didn't you tell me to get lost when I was interrogating you in my usual thoughtless way?'

For a crazy moment she thought he might kiss her, and a dizzy sensation made her sway. Then the feeling passed.

'Sometimes I can talk about it quite—quite calmly. Tonight for some reason I'm—I'm not too good.' She smiled up at him wanly. 'Maybe I shouldn't have drunk that whisky so fast.'

'Maybe I should have kept my big mouth shut. Do you want to sit down?'

'No, I'd rather go to bed, thanks. I really am tired.'

Calum kept hold of one of her arms as he walked her towards her room. His expression was mixed, as though he didn't want to feel sorry for Dot, yet couldn't help a sense of guilt at having upset her.

'Will you be all right?' he asked her as they paused at her doorway.

'I'll be fine,' she assured him. 'I was stupid. Forget it.'

He studied her briefly. 'You're upset at the thought of leaving Pearl.'

'A—a little.'

'But it isn't like a true bond,' he said, making it a statement rather than a question. 'She's just one of a long line of children you've cared for. You do it for the money. It's just a job to you, isn't it?'

Dot took a shaky breath, then nodded. 'Oh, yes,' she said with what passed for a smile, 'it's just a job to me. The money's what counts.'

Calum released her arm and stepped back, his face relapsing into its usual stony lines, like the crooked-nosed mask of a warrior. 'We'll talk about what to do tomorrow. Sleep well.'

He turned and walked away, and Dot closed the door and prepared for bed, feeling completely numb.

He was going to send her away. She felt it in her bones.

She got into bed and curled up on her side, her heart aching with a grief that had nothing to do with the sad memories Calum had invoked. She should never have come here. She should never have let Barbara Hescott inveigle her into accepting a situation she had known in her heart was as potentially cataclysmic as the San Andreas Fault.

'He's no angel, but he is an exceptional man...' 'Clara never understood him. Many women don't...' 'You have a lot in common with each other...'

Fragments of things Barbara had told her about Calum drifted through her thoughts. But Barbara's potted portrait of her nephew had carefully left out the really dangerous bits.

Barbara hadn't even answered her last couple of letters. Probably too ashamed of herself, Dot thought bitterly, to say anything.

Barbara should have known better! Should have stopped and thought out the implications before sending a woman like Dot into the lair of a man as devastatingly attractive as Calum. It had been a foregone conclusion that Dot would end up far too involved with both the child and the man for her own good. Dot had a vulnerable heart full of love, ready to give. Her life had been short on love and warmth, and those were things she prized above all else.

But the child was not hers, and the man saw her as nothing more than an unwelcome intrusion. Except once, when he had seen her as an available sex object. What could be in store for her except pain and loss?

Dot stared into the darkness with eyes that would have been too blurred with tears to see, even if the light had been on. What the hell did she care so much about Calum for, anyway? It wasn't as though he had ever shown her more than a few moments of lust in all the time she had known him.

Yes, he was handsome, but she had been with handsome men before, and had never had feelings like this!

The maelstrom inside her was too confused to analyse. But she could pick out individual strands, threads in the web that had enmeshed her heart.

Her feeling of empathy with him, that for all the differences between them they were two of a kind, people who had been hurt, and who shared much in common. Barbara had predicted that, but it was something that had taken Dot a long time to understand.

Far more immediate had been Calum's sexuality. That was something Dot had felt from the start, the potent, exciting appeal he exerted over her senses. There was a challenging yet fulfilling feel to him. When she looked at him, he seemed to fill all her expectations of a man, as though he had some psychic profile that matched a corresponding hollow in her own sensuality.

His intelligence, his ability to achieve and conquer, were things that any woman would have found attractive. But there were other, far less definable things that drew her to him. Like her feeling that, if only he would stop seeing her as an enemy——

She stopped her thoughts short, knowing the dangerous boundary between reality and fantasy. This was not a situation for fantasy on her part. Not any more.

The sweet scent of the chrysanthemums touched her senses.

It sometimes hurt so much to talk about the accident. It brought back the sick, uncomprehending misery of those weeks afterwards. She had been just old enough to feel real pain, too young to know any way of escaping it, and the feelings lingered in her. Even now, more than twelve years later, talking about it could take the breath from her lungs, the blood from her cheeks.

But she would willingly have gone through that painful remembrance again, just to see the hostility leave Calum's eyes for once, and see his mouth gentle into compassion.

When he had looked at her like that, just for that moment when she had thought he was going to kiss her lips, it was as though her heart had stopped.

She was thinking now of the intense, melting sweetness of those moments by the pool. What if she hadn't stopped him then? If she had let him make love to her that night, would he have felt any more warmly towards her? Would he have accepted her place in the family?

A high price to pay for a little warmth, she thought bitterly, turning on her other side. It wasn't warmth she had wanted, in any case. She had just wanted a truce with him, a cessation of hostilities. A normal relationship.

Well? What *was* a normal relationship between a single woman and the single man whose child she was caring for?

In the three months or so that she had known Calum, she had long since given up thinking in terms of normality.

Well, the saga was nearly over now. Tomorrow would, she felt ominously sure, bring a surgical end to her misery here.

CHAPTER SIX

DOT walked up from the lake, past the shops, lost in her thoughts. As always, her progress was accompanied by an endless chorus of friendly *konnichi-was* from people she met, but today her heart wasn't in the mood to appreciate Japanese politeness.

She had slept badly last night, and this morning had felt raw and tender inside. Any loud noise, she felt, would have her bursting into tears.

While Calum had driven Pearl into Tokyo to fit her out for the trip, Dot had taken herself for a long walk along the edge of the lake. The tranquillity of the snowy landscape had gone a long way towards instilling some calm into her unhappy thoughts, and she was feeling, if not happy, at least fatalistic as she made her way back to the house.

Calum and Pearl would be long back from the sports shop, and it was time to go and admire the gleaming new skis, boots, jackets, goggles, poles and hats that Pearl would have been equipped with this morning.

It would be Christmas in a week. She and Pearl had started making a Christmas tree, using a fir tree in a pretty ceramic jar, provided by Calum. They were decorating it with paper chains and various sparkling things that presented themselves as appropriate, but they still needed a star to go on top.

Christmas was a time she dreaded, because it brought her mother and father into her mind so much, provoking at least one tearful episode every year. She was just hoping that this year, with all the extra tensions,

124

she wouldn't start grizzling in front of everyone. Well, from Boxing Day until the ninth of January, she was going to have a fortnight all to herself, with nobody there to see whether she cried or not. Unless, of course, she had been sent home by then.

She had already started filling a stocking for Pearl, all too aware that she might soon be parting from the child.

But what to buy for Calum was an utter puzzle to her. He was a very rich and successful man, and seemed to have everything he wanted. And his tastes were so eclectic that she could hardly guess what would please him.

Yet she did want to please him, even if he was about to send her back home, and she didn't want to give something small and trivial. Questioning Oba-san had provoked only perplexity. Christmas was not a festival in Buddhist/Shinto Japan.

Dot knew that he loved *bonsai*, the tiny trees which the Japanese were so expert at dwarfing, and that he had an extensive collection. They could be formidably expensive things, costing hundreds of pounds, but so far that looked like the likeliest gift. She would go to a nursery this week, and pick one.

She walked up the drive, drinking in the beauty all around her with an ache in her heart, her breath clouding around her lips.

The red Porsche was in the garage. As soon as she got into the house, however, and sat down to take off her coat and exchange her boots for the indoor mules, she sensed that all was not well. She closed the inner door behind her, to be greeted by Hanako, who sank to her knees to give Dot a full, old-fashioned forehead-on-floor bow, something that indicated great upset.

'What is it?' Dot demanded, helping Hanako to her feet. The girl's face was a mask of woe.

'Pearl-san very sick this morning,' she told her, her eyes filling with tears.

'Sick?'

'Shouting and crying,' Hanako nodded miserably.

'Oh,' Dot said, painful understanding dawning on her, 'that kind of sick. Where is she now?'

'In bed. Calum-san call doctor for medicine.'

Dot hurried to Pearl's room, her heart in her mouth. The child was asleep on her side, but her scarlet, tear-stained cheeks bore ample evidence of the storm that had passed. The dark hair was tumbled across the pillow.

There were some broken toys on the floor. A little strip of sticking-plaster on one of Pearl's outflung hands showed where she must have scratched herself in her tantrum.

She was obviously sedated, which made Dot grimace. That hadn't been necessary. But of course, they wouldn't have known what to do.

Well, she would have to face Calum.

As she passed the kitchen she heard sniffling, and popped in to find Oba-san crying quietly over the lunch.

'It's all right, Oba-san,' said Dot, comforting the housekeeper with a hug. 'Pearl isn't sick. She just lost her temper.'

'Everybody very frightened,' Oba-san said, giving her a hug in return. '*Shimata*—so sorry to be crying.'

'It doesn't matter.'

'So glad you back. Gardener ran to fetch you, but couldn't find you.'

Dot cursed her untimely absence. 'I was down by the lake. Where's Calum? In his study?'

'*Hai.*'

She went to find him, not looking forward to the interview. He was standing at the window, hands in the pockets of his slacks, staring out at the snow. Obviously expensive, Pearl-sized ski equipment was scattered all over the floor. He didn't turn to face her.

'What happened?' she asked quietly.

'It was so sudden,' he said, sounding tired. 'One minute she was happy and laughing. She was trying her skis on. She couldn't get the buckle fastened, such a minor thing, but suddenly she just...exploded. I've never seen anything like it.'

'Yes,' Dot said heavily, 'it can be frightening. And often it's some tiny little annoyance that sets it off. Hanako says you called the doctor.'

'You weren't to be found.' He turned to look at her at last, his face stony. 'And we couldn't stop her. She was throwing things, kicking, screaming...the gist of it being that she wasn't going to Hakuba without you.'

Dot let that one ride. 'What did the doctor give her?'

'Some herbal tea—valerian. She didn't drink much of it—by the time he got here, she was exhausted, and ready to fall asleep of her own accord.'

Calum walked over to her and grasped her arms in his hands. Last night it had been a gesture almost of comfort, but today his fingers bit into her flesh like steel, making her gasp. His eyes burned into hers, like the blue flames of burning copper.

'What kind of witch are you?' he demanded in a fierce undertone. 'What spell are you weaving round us?'

'I'm not weaving any spell! Please let me go—you're hurting me!'

He released her with an obvious effort. 'What the hell am I supposed to do about you?' he asked, in the same rough voice, though whether he was addressing her or talking to himself Dot did not know. 'Barbara said you'd be a blessing, but you've turned out to be a curse instead! Your influence was supposed to get weaker, not stronger.'

'Then you'd better do what you said last night,' said Dot in a low voice, 'and get rid of me.'

'And have my daughter screaming herself into fits every time a buckle won't fasten?' He walked over to his desk, grim-faced. Every inch of his tall, hard frame seemed to be bristling with electricity. 'You were a mistake,' he said harshly. 'But now is obviously not the time to rectify it.'

'On the contrary,' she retorted, 'what you said last night was quite right. I've been thinking about it all morning. With the holiday coming up, and Barbara due here in February, it's probably the most suitable time to make a break.' She swallowed. 'I'm quite ready to go back to England when you've set off for Hakuba.'

He glanced at her angrily. 'Oh? Pearl doesn't mean that much to you, then?'

'Pearl means——' She had to stop herself. 'Pearl means a lot to me,' she said tensely, her clear grey eyes meeting his. 'But you are her father, and also my employer. I'm not going to stand in your way, whatever your decision is.'

A beautifully inlaid curved *samurai* sword always lay on his desk, and Calum picked it up now in both hands, as if seeing it for the first time.

'I'm not in an ideal position to make decisions,' he said brusquely. 'It seems to me I'm between the devil and the deep blue sea. Whatever I do will be wrong.'

He dropped the sword again, with a clatter that made her jump, and turned to her.

'Have you nothing to say?'

'I've said what I think. That I should go home and start looking for another job, while you look for another governess.'

'I'll have no more governesses,' he said grimly. 'Like wives, one is quite enough.' He surveyed her figure broodingly. 'Do you play squash?'

'Well, I used to,' Dot said, taken aback by the question.

His eyes glittered. 'Good. I feel like a quick game. We'll go down to the club.'

'Shouldn't we stay here——?'

'Pearl will sleep until dinnertime. And I'm too tense to concentrate right now. Come.'

Dot's heart sank. If she had been a man, she suspected that in his present mood Calum would have enjoyed laying into her with his fists; squash was very likely going to be a thinly disguised form of aggression.

Which was exactly the way it turned out.

They drove down to the sports club which overlooked the lake, where Calum played, and easily found a spare court at that time of the afternoon.

The scene of her castigation was a beautifully new court, with a pale wood floor and a glass wall for spectators. When they started to play, Calum's release of energy was explosive. Dot didn't even get a racket to his first three services. She was no match at all for his trained, hostile power, and within a few minutes she knew that he was coldly setting out to humiliate her.

She was playing with a racket he had lent her, and she was wearing a T-shirt and a tracksuit bottom that was far too hot for the game. She grew steadily more red-faced and sweaty as she chased around the court, feeling like a salmon hooked by some particularly sadistic angler. He was hitting the ball with venomous accuracy and force, his dark face concentrated into a mask of application to his purpose.

They played three more sets, watched by a silent audience of Japanese, at the end of which Dot was trembling with tiredness and anger. She would have minded it less if Calum had actually struck her. This methodical, brutal punishment had been utterly uncalled for.

'That'll do,' he said at last, not looking at her as he went to fetch his kit. His tone was so exactly that of the headmaster who has applied correction that Dot had to restrain herself from hurling her racket at his broad back.

The bastard! she thought as she stood under the shower, her eyes squeezed shut. The utter bastard! She was going to ache for days after this. Was this his idea of justice? To crush her pride, just because his daughter showed some love for her?

The selfish, overbearing, male chauvinist *pig*!

She limped to her clothes, dripping and spluttering, and towelled herself dry. In the full-length mirror she caught sight of her naked body. There was a bruise on her hip and elbow. She faced herself, taking stock of her slim, elegant lines, her pretty breasts and long legs. She was a person. She mattered.

Well, she was not going to have her pride crushed by Calum!

She dried her hair, applied lipstick to her full mouth, and went out to meet him, tightly determined not to show the white feather. He was waiting for her in the lobby, moodily examining the notice board, his kitbag in one brown hand.

'I enjoyed that,' she said firmly, walking up to him.

He turned to look at her, and she met his eyes with a bright smile. His face was expressionless.

'Is that so?'

'Yes,' she confirmed. 'The exercise has done me so much good. I haven't felt this relaxed in ages.' She stretched out a painful arm to show how much she had benefited. 'I could do with improving my game too. Maybe we could have a game every week.'

Calum blinked. Then, reluctantly, a slow smile made its way across his mouth, turning his eyes from the colour of a winter fjord to summer-sky blue. 'You've got more spirit than I bargained for,' he said gently. 'I don't know why I did that to you.'

'To stop yourself from punching me in the mouth, I suppose,' Dot said, deadpan.

His big shoulders slumped slightly, and his smile faded. 'Maybe. I shouldn't have done it, and I'm sorry.'

'Two apologies in one month?' She wasn't letting him off the hook that easily. 'You really must be slipping!'

'Come on. You've made me feel rotten. Now don't push it.' He reached out and relieved her of her kitbag. 'How would you like to sit on real chairs, at a real table, and have a real cup of coffee?'

Her expression told him how she viewed that proposal, and he led her to the American-style restaurant, where he bought her not only the coffee but a real toasted cheese and ham sandwich, something she had been craving for weeks.

They sat by the window, overlooking the grey sheet of the lake that stretched out to the snowy, misty mountains beyond, and talked about Pearl.

'It's an upsetting thing to see your child behave like that,' Calum said quietly. 'You forget how much you care for them until you see them rolling around the floor, screaming. If you'd only been there——'

'I'm sorry I wasn't,' Dot said quietly.

He dismissed her apology with a gesture. 'I didn't know what to do. She was only a baby when Clara and I divorced. I feel I've missed so much of her childhood. If I hadn't, I might know her better.' He shrugged. 'I just have to hope that I'm doing what's right by her—for better or worse.'

'Oh, I think you're having a good influence on each other.'

Calum met her eyes measuringly, his gaze as always making her heart constrict. 'In what way has Pearl had an influence over me?'

'You've changed since she came. Slowed down.'

'Slowed down?' he echoed, looking disgusted. 'What, like an unwound clock?'

'I told you you must be slipping.' Dot finished her sandwich, and dabbed her greasy fingers regretfully. It would be a long time before she saw the next toasted cheese and ham sandwich.

What she had said was true. Calum almost always came home for lunch these days, and his formerly hectic nightlife had dwindled to the once or twice-weekly dinner party at home. Not that he was exactly domesticated, but she was growing accustomed to having him around in the evenings for a change.

'I meant that your life seems a little less hectic these days. More normal, now.'

Calum grunted. 'You should have seen my marriage! We were out every night till dawn, usually later. I used to go straight to the lab in a dinner jacket sometimes, work all day, break for a shower and a bite, then be straight out again.'

'You weren't doing so badly when I—when Pearl arrived,' Dot said drily.

'Oh, I'm a reformed character,' he smiled. 'It was having Pearl that really changed me.' His smile faded, and his face became bleak again. 'Unfortunately, it didn't change Clara.'

Dot stretched her aching legs out. 'How long were you married?' she asked casually.

'Two years before Pearl. A year after that, until we broke up, and then the divorce. Three, in all.'

'And you were happy until Pearl came along?'

'Not really. We were infatuated rather than in love. I was only twenty-six when we married, a boy wonder dazzled by my own success, and ready to be dazzled by any pretty face that came along. Pearl just showed up the cracks, that's all.'

'She was very wrong to keep you from seeing Pearl.' Dot knew she was on shaky ground, but Calum's formidable guard seemed to be down for once. 'No matter what had happened over the divorce, it was cruel to Pearl as well as you.'

'Clara wasn't a very moral person,' Calum commented. Dot watched the bitter expression cross his mouth, as it always did when he mentioned his ex-wife.

'Maybe you're going to bite my head off for saying this,' she said warily, 'but last night it occurred to me that you might have the wrong idea about me and Pearl. That you might be unnecessarily... well, jealous.'

She had expected an eruption, but it didn't come. He stared out across the lake. 'That morning,' he began hesitantly, 'in the airport... you must have thought my behaviour pretty harsh.'

'We were neither of us in a very good mood.'

'Everything had happened so frustratingly. First of all, I couldn't get away from my work to come and fetch the kid. I was in the middle of a critical period, and there was no way I could leave the office without causing chaos. I had to let Barbara arrange it all in London. Then, on the day you arrived, I was a bundle of nerves.'

'You?'

'I wanted everything to be perfect. But first that fool ran into my car in the middle of town. And then, when

I finally got to the airport, Pearl was sedated, and couldn't even say hello to me... I know it sounds pathetic, but I was so disappointed.'

'Oh, Calum,' Dot sighed remorsefully, 'I've cursed that pill so many times!'

'You should have cursed me instead. I was willing enough for the doctor to give her that herbal tea when she had the tantrum. I realise now that you did it for Pearl's sake, not for your own convenience. I wasn't a very experienced parent at that stage, Dot.'

She took a deep breath, but Calum didn't seem to notice her emotion.

'It was a weird sort of day. I had a kind of awful feeling that history was repeating itself.' He hesitated, obviously finding the words difficult. 'When I first saw you, sitting there with Pearl in your arms——'

'What?' Dot asked, as he stopped.

'Well...' He looked uncomfortable. 'Clara had curly black hair, a bit like yours. She used to hold Pearl in that way, sometimes, staring into space. You even have the same kind of figure, tall and slender.' His dark blue eyes met hers. 'Except that Clara's face never wore an expression like the one you're wearing now. Are you upset?'

'Not at all,' she lied. 'Do I—do I still remind you of her?'

'No,' he said flatly. 'There were never two more different women born.'

He didn't elaborate, but she chose to take it as some sort of compliment.

'It wasn't jealousy,' he went on. 'I guess it was a kind of haunting. Marriage is a funny thing,' he said, eyes on her. 'Have you never been tempted to holy wedlock?'

'Not so far,' Dot smiled.

'Never once?'

Under that searching gaze, she felt her poise falter. 'Well,' she said, dropping her thick lashes, 'there was once someone...'

'Things didn't work out?' he asked, with unexpected gentleness.

'Not exactly.' Dot folded her napkin into squares. 'He was...much older than me. He was supposed to be divorcing his wife. But in the end he went back to her.'

Calum's dark eyebrows rose. 'That doesn't sound like your scene at all.'

She pulled a face. 'I suppose it wasn't. But I fancied myself in love with him.' She was remembering that summer, and the endless hurt and confusion that Jack had put her through. There was no earthly reason why she should tell Calum about it, but she found that she was doing so, anyway.

'I was twenty-two and Jack was in his forties, and I suppose he was playing a not very nice game with me.' She gave Calum a brief glance. 'With hindsight, I think he was indulging his fantasies. His marriage was going through a bad patch, and he was distracting himself with the dream that he would leave his wife, and set up a new life with a much younger woman.'

'It sounds as though you ended up rather badly hurt,' Calum said neutrally.

'I did,' she nodded. 'I went through a lot of heartache that was quite unnecessary.' She laughed briefly. 'Juvenile, but painful. Jack was a man who wouldn't get off the fence. The trouble was, he still wanted to fish on both sides of it.'

Jack had never relinquished his marriage. When Dot had met him, he had told her he was divorced. It was only later that he let drop that the divorce was still in progress. And only much later still that she had learned that there were no divorce proceedings at all, and that what he really had in mind was an extra-marital affair, with no strings.

At the time she had been fresh out of university, working in her first job as a governess, with a rather difficult French family in central London. The pressures on her, from all directions, had been enormous, and she had been lucky to escape a nervous collapse of some kind.

She told Calum about her feelings for Jack Taunton, made stronger and less controllable by the years of loneliness she had endured since losing her parents. About the way she had cried all night sometimes. About the way she had anguished over him for three months. The way she had been enmeshed with countless strands of guilt. Guilt over Jack, guilt over his wife, guilt over the whole ugly mess of a three-sided relationship she had been trapped into.

She also told him about the pressure Jack had put on her to move into a flat with him, and the way he had made her suffer when she had refused to do so until his divorce was final.

And in the end, she told him about the way it had all come to nothing, with Jack reconciling himself to his marriage, and treating Dot as though she, and not he, had been the guilty one, the marriage-breaker.

Calum had listened in silence. When she had finished, he drained his cup, and stared out of the window.

'So you never lived with him?'

'No.'

'And you've never lived with any man since? Or had any kind of serious relationship with any man?'

'Well,' she explained with an unsteady laugh, 'I was rather put off relationships. Serious ones, I mean. I've had plenty of men friends since Jack, but . . .'

'But you don't let them go too far,' he supplied for her. He had so exactly guessed her attitude that she said nothing, just stared down at the napkin she kept folding into smaller and smaller squares.

His strong, tanned hand reached out, stilling her fretful fingers. His touch was warm and firm.

'You're a virgin,' he said softly. 'Aren't you?'

Dot felt her cheeks flame hotly. She forced herself to look up and meet his eyes. 'Yes,' she said in a muted voice.

Calum stared at her oval face, his expression unreadable. Then he withdrew his hand.

'You didn't tell me that, that night by the pool.'

'You didn't ask.'

'A man doesn't usually ask that question of a woman who——' He bit back whatever he was going to say. Dot couldn't tell whether he was angry with her or not, but she thought he might be. When he spoke again, his voice was harsh. 'I might have found a lot of things about you easier to understand if I'd known that.'

'You talk as though I were some kind of mystery,' she said, trying to smile it off.

'Some kind of mystery,' he repeated drily. 'You could say that.'

'I thought it showed.' She was flushing again. 'Being—being a virgin, I mean. I thought men could tell that kind of thing.'

'How?' he grated. 'By the unicorn laying its head in your lap? By the little neon sign over your head, reading *"Caution, Maiden"*?'

'Just by—well, by the way I was.'

'You're not the blushing, virginal type, Dorothy.' He shook his head wryly, as though still trying to digest what she had told him. 'You're articulate and adult and very well able to fend for yourself. In fact, you can be so downright bloody-minded at times that you drive me to distraction!'

She was surprised out of her mortification. 'Is *that* the way you see me?'

'Why?' he asked sardonically. 'Do you see yourself as a shy and melting waif?'

'Well, I think I'm not very assertive. Not with you, anyway,' she added meaningfully. 'Not assertive enough by half.'

'Just do me a favour,' Calum rasped, 'and don't get any more assertive! I don't think I could bear it. You're a rose with too many thorns.'

'That means a rose not worth picking,' Dot said. If it was a query, she got her answer.

'You're right,' he said drily. 'I prefer my roses thornless. And I prefer my women experienced.'

She looked away to hide the hurt in her eyes.

Calum rose to his feet, indicating that it was time to go back.

By the time they got back to the house, Pearl was up and about, and looking as though butter wouldn't melt in her mouth. Nobody referred to the tantrum, though Oba-san and Hanako treated her rather gingerly. They had an early dinner, and then went to the sitting-area. Calum had been talking about problems he faced at work, when his attention was caught by Pearl, sprawled on her tummy by the fireside, with her books scattered round her.

Surprised, he stopped talking to listen while she flipped the pages, reciting the words to herself.

'And, Cat, Bat, Dog...'

Dot watched Calum's expression without saying anything. He had hardly been aware of the progress his daughter was making, and this was obviously the first time he had seen her in action.

He turned to stare at Dot, his eyes narrowed. 'Is that real?' he demanded, as Pearl moved on to other games.

'Yes.' Dot smiled slightly. 'She can read about two dozen words already. Including her own name, though that's definitely the only five-letter word she can manage so far!'

He was silent for a long while, studying her face with intense eyes, until she started to colour in embarrassment.

'You've been extremely clever,' he said slowly, the frown on his forehead uncreasing.

'I'm not the clever one.' She nodded at Pearl, who was lying on her back, going through her words again. 'She's a quick learner. Pretty soon she'll start to be able to read simple words she hasn't seen before.'

'Yet I've heard that mothers shouldn't try and teach their children to read,' Calum said, glancing at Pearl.

The words gave her a strange feeling. 'I'm not her mother,' she reminded him gently. 'I'm her governess.'

Calum looked at her sharply. His face wore an odd expression for a moment, as though he had almost forgotten who she was.

Dot felt a pang of pain. Had he, once again, been imagining it was Clara, and not herself, who sat here by his side? It wasn't a hard mistake to make. The situation was so like that of a normal family evening...

Calum rose and scooped Pearl up in his arms.

'Who's a clever little button, then?' he grinned, hoisting her up until she squealed. 'Come on, read me some more words.' His delight was unmistakable.

Even if he sent her back to England, Dot thought with satisfaction, at least she had achieved something with this child. And he knew it.

The next morning, over breakfast, Calum glanced at Dot casually.

'I take it you can ski?'

'Not very well,' she said hesitantly.

'What does not very well mean?'

'Well—I once spent a fortnight skiing in Val d'Aosta with some friends. I'd just learned the basics when I did my knee in. Why?'

'Because you're coming to Hakuba with us.'

Dot was startled. 'I really don't think——'

His eyes raked her up and down assessingly. 'You're fit enough, slender though you are,' he said, as though he hadn't heard her objection. 'You put up a good show at the courts yesterday. You'll manage.'

'But you can't be thinking of taking me with you, just because Pearl threw a tantrum!'

'I rang the hotel in Hakuba last night,' he told her. 'By some miracle, they've got an extra room. It's a double, so you'll have plenty of room. I imagine the impropriety of a single maiden in a double room won't disturb your delicate sensibilities?'

Dot stared at him. 'Then—you're not sending me back to England?'

'No,' he said sharply. 'I've decided—you're coming to Hakuba.' His eyes glittered. 'With any luck, you might just disappear into a snowdrift for ever, and solve all my problems.'

'Well, I could solve all your problems by simply going back home,' argued Dot, pushing away her plate. 'This is silly. I haven't any gear, even if I wanted to come—which I don't.'

'And it'll be too late to hire any,' he commented, his mouth twisting. 'This is going to work out expensive. We don't have much time, either. Ah well, in for a penny...'

He went over to the telephone, keying in a number with aggressive punches of his forefinger.

'Ryoko? Listen. Something's come up at home, and I don't know when I'll make it into the office this morning. If I'm not in by noon, will you leave all the folders on my desk? And ask Watanabe to double-check that program. I'll handle anything left over this afternoon.' He replaced the receiver and jerked a thumb at Dot. 'Get a coat.'

'Where are we going?' she queried.

'Back to the sports shop,' he said briskly. 'We've got some shopping to do.'

It was futile to protest. Calum's mind was made up, and her resistance only earned her a stinging rebuke, and a snapped, 'Will you damned well do as I say for once?'

They drove into Tokyo, parking in the outskirts, and taking a taxi into the congested centre.

Dot stared at the towering cityscape, with its strange mixture of the classically Japanese and the aggressively American. So she wasn't banished back to England yet. But what on earth could Calum have in mind? After the skiing trip, the situation would be just as bad as ever, if not worse.

He would either have to accept that his daughter needed Dot, and ask her to stay on, or he would have to harden his heart and get rid of her. There was no middle way. She herself couldn't hold back with the child—that would be cruel—and Pearl needed a mother figure just as much as she needed her father.

It would have been a difficult situation if Calum Hescott had been the mildest and most gentle of men. Given that he was about as mild and gentle as the fire-breathing dragon on his favourite kimono, the predicament was very real.

Skiing was evidently huge business in Japan. The immense shop was better equipped with winter sports gear than anything Dot had ever seen. Everything from children's skis and sleds to fully rigged Olympic toboggans was on display, and the clothing section was like a whole department store in itself.

It scarcely eased Dot's tension that Calum was intent that she should have only the best equipment available. It was in vain for her to move over towards the cheapest skis; he had an assistant come and measure her proportions with great care, and picked a pair of slick red skis that were far better than she could ever need. Similarly elegant ski-poles followed, with red leather gloves.

And when they walked through to find some clothing, he went straight to the rails where the costliest, down-filled jackets hung.

Dot was acutely aware of his dark eyes on her as she tried on several. Nothing would have given her more pleasure than this extravagant shopping spree in normal circumstances. But the way Calum never took his eyes off her, his tanned face mask-like, was very offputting. His presence made sure that the busy assistants somehow found time to flutter round her, bowing and complimenting her on her appearance, so that she felt even more the focus of attention.

He was dressing a plaything for his daughter, she thought at one point. Making sure that the governess's appearance didn't let him down on the slopes. Well, what the hell? If he wanted to spend a fortune on her, why should she feel guilty? Let him do as he pleased!

She settled on an emerald green jacket that was not only deliciously light and warm, but looked sensational on her slender figure. That was the keynote for three or four other items, like a woolly hat, ski pants, and something Calum insisted on, a warm tracksuit.

The shop was crowded, and Dot had to queue for a changing cubicle. With usual Japanese unselfconsciousness about such things, they were shared by men and women.

Finally in a cubicle by herself, Dot started trying on the armful of expensive clothing she had brought in with her. The tracksuits were proving rather more difficult than the jacket had done, as Japanese proportions seemed to be very different from Western ones. The ones with arms and legs long enough tended to be far too baggy.

After ten minutes, the curtain was suddenly swept aside, and Calum looked in, a pale grey tracksuit over one arm. 'This is supposed to be an American size,' he said. 'Try it on.'

Dot was wearing only a tracksuit bottom and a lacy, see-through bra that cupped her small breasts provocatively. She saw Calum's blue eyes drop to her bosom, the pupils dark discs. A sudden memory of that night by the pool made her flush hotly.

Trying not to react stupidly, she took the garment he offered her, and pulled the jacket over her head. As she shook her black hair free, she knew that he had watched the way the movement had tautened her breasts against the lace. She straightened the arms, which seemed about right, and then met his eyes in the mirror.

'The top fits, at any rate,' she said, not wanting to sound flustered by his presence. 'If you'll just shut the curtain, I'll try the pants.'

His eyes glinted. 'Sure,' he said flatly, and stepped into the cubicle with her.

As he shut the curtain behind them, Dot's flush deepened.

'I didn't mean like that,' she said shortly. 'I meant with you on the *outside*.'

'I've seen a great deal more of you than is on show right now,' he reminded her acidly. 'Don't be such a puritan!'

Dot hesitated. He was paying a fortune for all this stuff, but that didn't give him the right to embarrass her like this. However, it was pointless to argue with him in his present mood.

Stiffly, she turned her back on him, pulled off one pair of tracksuit bottoms, and slipped as neatly as she could into the other pair. The most he could have seen was the backs of her slim legs, for a few seconds.

'Well?' she asked pointedly, turning to him. 'Does it meet with your approval?'

He studied her, his gaze moving in a slow downward sweep. 'Yes,' he said at last, 'that looks right.'

'Then I'd like this one,' she said. 'And please, *please* don't buy me anything else. I've got far more than I'll ever need already. I'm sure I could have hired skis, and with what I had at home I'd have been perfectly adequately equipped for Hakuba.'

'It isn't worth buying cheap skiing equipment. The best is warmer, safer, and longer lasting.'

'It only has to last a fortnight,' Dot reminded him pointedly.

'Oh, I'm sure you'll find some rich young Romeo who'll want to show you off in all the smart winter resorts one day,' he said sardonically. 'Your nice green jacket will last you through an Alpine affair or two.'

'I don't have affairs,' she said irritably, 'Alpine or otherwise. I wish you hadn't spent so much money on me.'

He smiled tightly. 'You're a beautiful woman... *Dot.* I've rather enjoyed dressing you up.'

Discomfited, Dot turned away. 'Well,' she observed, 'it's been an expensive exercise for you.'

'Call this your Christmas present,' he shrugged. 'You needed the right kind of clothing. Hakuba is the St Moritz of Japan.'

'But I'm hardly in the Japanese jet-set!'

'But you'll be with me. And at least I won't be embarrassed to be seen with you now.'

'Is that why you've done all this?' she asked quietly, folding the rejected clothing and getting her street clothes from underneath.

'Of course. Everyone will assume you're my mistress,' he said with what might have been caustic humour. 'I wouldn't want them to think me mean in my *amours*.'

The words cut into her like knives. 'I'd like to change now, please,' she said coldly.

Calum took a black curl of her hair in his fingers and caressed it with his thumb, as though assessing the dark sheen. 'You don't like me to say things like that, do you?' he challenged her, his mouth curving into a taunting smile.

'Considering the relationship between us, I don't think I do, no.'

'Am I too old?'

'Yes,' snapped Dot. 'You're too everything. Yesterday you were going to sack me, and today you're buying me the most expensive skiing gear that can be had in Tokyo. I like things steady, Calum.' She glared up at him, her grey eyes glittering. 'I like to know where I'm at. What I hate is being kicked around like a football——'

She broke off on a gasp as Calum's mouth closed on hers. His kiss was fierce, burningly intense. His arms claimed her hungrily, obviously unaware that their formidable strength was crushing the breath out of her. She whimpered in pain, the sound lost against Calum's mouth.

But he must have heard it, or sensed the way her trapped arms tensed, because the iron bands relaxed at once, and the plundering mouth gentled. She felt his hands move up under her tracksuit, caressing the cool, naked skin of her back, his tongue sliding between her lips to savour the sweetness of her inner mouth.

Dot's heart was suddenly pounding. He had hurt her so badly over the past few weeks, yet one touch of his lips seemed to turn all that pain into something else, something that burned in her like a bonfire. Her craving for him was surging through her veins to impel her against him. The alchemy of sex was turning dislike into hunger, aggression into desire.

'Dot,' Calum muttered harshly, drawing back and looking down into her drowned eyes. 'You're too damned insignificant to be called Dorothy. I'm going to call you Dot from now on...'

He was kissing her again, whispering her name, his hands on her hips pulling her against him. Her emotion was out of control, her heart feeling as though it would burst inside her.

'Don't,' she cried out, her pulses pounding insanely. 'Calum, no!'

'Any problem?' An assistant peered into the cubicle, her smooth face puckered in concern at Dot's cry. Her almond eyes widened, then she bowed her way out, giggling.

Dot pushed Calum away, suddenly feeling suffocatingly hot. 'Get out of here!' she snapped at him, dragging the dark hair away from her feverish face. 'You have no right to do this to me!'

'Sorry,' he said starkly. 'From time to time my overheated imagination runs away with me. I imagine that there's some slight response in you, which of course is impossible. Isn't it?'

'If you've got the wrong impression about me, that isn't my fault!'

'Quite. I forget that you're actually an accurate plastic replica of a woman, programmed to do a limited number of basic tasks.' He took a harsh, deep breath. 'Which don't include physical contact with the opposite sex. Well, I'm sorry my attentions drive you to screaming for help.'

'I didn't mean to——'

But he had pushed his way through the curtains, leaving her to change alone.

Oh, damn. Dot sagged against the wall, cursing her own inexperience. Why did she always fight him off? Feeling about him the way she did, his kiss was what she craved, more than the air she breathed.

Yet it was always wrong, in the wrong place or at the wrong time. And she always pushed him away, hurting his feelings, driving a wedge between them. No wonder he found her hard to understand, and thought her bloody-minded.

How was he to know that his touch was simply too much for her?

How was he, an experienced and sensual man, to understand that being made love to in a public place like this huge shop was something that made her soul quail in dismay?

She changed, her heart aching.

CHAPTER SEVEN

A LETTER from Barbara Hescott arrived for Dot at last, on Christmas Eve. It was long, full of praises about Pearl's progress, and full of news about London doings.

Only on the last page did she turn to the subject of Dot's relations with Calum.

> I can't deny that I anticipated some of the problems you're having with my dear nephew. I knew that he was a bit of a misogynist after Clara, and he can certainly be an utter brute at times. His father, my eldest brother, was just as bad.
>
> I thought of warning you, several times. But what could I say, my love? If I'd put you off, you might not have taken on the job, and you've been the perfect person for Pearl. Thank goodness you went to the child, Dorothy—you've been her salvation, and I shall always be irretrievably in your debt.
>
> Anyway, in the end, I decided to say nothing, guessing that you could cope with whatever Calum threw at you. I sincerely hope you're giving him as good in return, which is the only way to deal with Calum. But I have to plead guilty to deception, deceit, guile, false witness, suppression of the truth—I'll have to go and fetch my Thesaurus to find enough words of self-blame!

Dot smiled at that, and read on.

However, I have to point out one or two things. One is that if Calum really thought you were a fool and a nuisance, he would treat you with icy politeness. He's only really rude to people he thinks something of.

Dot pulled a face, thinking she could do without that kind of respect. The logic of that theory escaped her. It was worse than a Zen parable.

The other is that you're an extremely attractive woman, and Calum is susceptible to attractive women, to say the least. I know he wouldn't lay a finger on you...

Dot pulled an even sourer face...

...but your presence at Chinsanzo will certainly have troubled the surface of his waters, so to speak. So think about that, and try to forgive my nephew the pig!

Anyway, I'm looking forward so much to being with you in February. We'll join in feminine solidarity against male chauvinism, wherever we find it.

There were a few more paragraphs of consolation, ending, 'Hope you all have a lovely Christmas and New Year. My kisses and best wishes to you all. Much love, Barbara.'

Dot's feelings weren't a great deal eased by Barbara's letter. Things had gone so far between her and Calum by now that she knew she would never be able to tell Barbara what had really happened. And Barbara was obviously unaware that Dot's job was still hanging by a thread. What would she say if Calum did end up by sacking her?

Well, Pearl was Calum's daughter. What could Barbara say? The prospect of having Barbara on her side in February was certainly consoling—if she was still here by February. But Dot didn't kid herself that Barbara, or anyone else, would really be able to save her from the hurt that Calum could dish out. Calum was a law unto himself.

Dot went to her room and wrote Barbara a reply, sticking to the facts this time, and leaving out the complaints. She was feeling rather ashamed of having poured out her heart to Barbara like that, and resolved not to do it again. Sink or swim, she had to fend for herself.

On Christmas morning Dot was awakened by a pyjamaed Pearl, pink with excitement, who burst into her room at six-thirty.

'There *is* Father Christmas in Japan!' she squealed, showing Dot her bulging Christmas stocking.

There had been some doubt about whether Father Christmas's beat covered Japan. As the Father—or Mother—Christmas who had hung that very stocking above Pearl's bed at one o'clock that morning, Dot was feeling rather bleary.

'Happy Christmas, darling,' she said giving Pearl a hug. 'Don't scream like that, you'll wake your father.'

But Pearl, who had been in soaring spirits ever since being told that Dot was coming to Hakuba after all, was not to be restrained this morning. Squatting on Dot's white futon, she started hauling out the prettily wrapped gifts, her blue eyes huge and shining with delight. Dot couldn't help loving her as she squeaked in joy over her haul—little puzzles, packets of sweets, the odd tangerine, a myriad of the superb little toys that Tokyo shops so excelled in. So intense was her delight that it was almost impossible to get her to brush her teeth and hair,

or to organise her to the breakfast table. Only the hint
that other and larger delights might be waiting under the
Christmas tree seemed to produce any effect.

Calum was studying the newspapers in the dining-area,
wearing dark slacks and a black polo-neck. His eyes glittered like sapphires at Pearl's joyful entrance, and he
swept her up in his strong arms to give her a hug and a
whirl round before setting her down.

Dot walked up to him as unselfconsciously as she
could, and kissed his cheek briefly.

'Happy Christmas,' she wished him formally.

It was hard to stay cool, however, as Pearl pounced
on the heap of presents under the tree, whooping. She
squatted to examine the cards attached, running her
finger along the writing.

'P-E-A-R-L,' she read unhesitatingly. 'That's me!'

She plunged into the wrapping, staring in delight at
the Noah's Ark which Dot had bought her, its innards
filled with pairs of brightly coloured animals.

There was also another huge teddy from her father,
and a variety of books and pretty clothes to be mar-
velled over. Not all the presents, however, were for Pearl.
There was a beautiful pale yellow *obi* for Hanako, and
an embroidered shawl for Oba-san that was, to Dot's
eyes, a miracle of needlework.

Calum appeared slightly taken aback to find that the
large red box with the gold ribbon was marked with his
name.

'From Dot,' he read, and glanced at her briefly before
unravelling the tape.

Dot waited with bated breath. She hadn't ever found
out just how much he had spent on her in the ski-shop,
but it had certainly come to hundreds of pounds. That
had hardened her decision that she wanted to buy him
something he would really appreciate for Christmas.

It had taken three visits to the bonsai nursery to pick the right tree, and a fourth to select the right container for it, an antique glazed *tokoname* dish with tiny, beautiful legs.

The tree was a juniper, an evergreen conifer. It was three hundred and seventy years old, and it was two feet high. Dot had picked it because it was the most beautiful tree there, and because no other bonsai in the nursery had filled her with such a sense of wonder and awe. It had cost her a sum of money she would never have dreamed of laying out on anything for herself, but Calum paid her more money than she knew what to do with, and the nurseryman had assured her that it was a specimen to grace the most serious of collections.

Calum pushed the wrapping paper aside, opened the box, and looked in.

If Dot had expected an emphatic reaction, she was disappointed. Calum's tanned face was expressionless, almost blank.

With great care he lifted the bonsai tree out of its box and placed it on the table in front of him, staring at it with dark blue eyes.

The juniper was a magnificent thing, its needles an intense green, with a trunk as gnarled and full of life as the hugest forest giant. Even Pearl, not noted as a botanist, was awestruck.

It was a long time before Calum looked up at her.

'Did they tell you how old it was?' he asked quietly. She told him.

'It's beautiful,' he said, speaking as though with an effort. 'I shall always prize it. Thank you.'

'I'm glad you like it,' she said lightly. But the look in his eyes had hit her like a blow to the heart.

'There's one left,' Pearl pointed out in excitement. 'It says D-O-T. That's you!'

The card was written in Calum's black scrawl, and Dot took the long, flat parcel with a grimace. 'I've already had so many costly presents from you,' she protested. 'You shouldn't have!'

'There has to be something left for Christmas Day,' he said with a shrug.

She unwrapped the flat box and lifted the lid.

Now it was her turn to look blank. It was a rope of pearls, exquisitely graded from specimens no bigger than tears to glowing pink orbs almost the size of her little fingernail. She lifted it out, the smooth pearls caressing her fingers, and stared at it, stunned. The slight unevennesses told her these were real pearls, not cultured ones, and worth a fortune.

Coming from any other man, this wouldn't be a present. It would be a declaration of love.

'A little thank-you,' he said casually, 'for looking after my Pearl so well.'

Dot's eyes were blurring with tears. To her dismay, there were no words, only choking sobs. She fled from the room before she disgraced herself utterly, and hid in her bedroom. Damn him, *damn* him! Why did he always reduce her to ashes when she least wanted it?

She was still flushed and red-eyed when her door slid open to reveal Calum. His expression was rather tense than otherwise.

'Breakfast's been burning while you've been having your cadenza,' he said shortly. 'Are you quite finished now?'

'Sorry,' Dot said weakly. 'I don't know what came over me. Calum, thank you so much for the pearls. I——'

'I don't want thanks,' he said shortly, cutting through her words.

'But they're so beautiful——'

'You shouldn't have bought that tree,' he went on harshly. 'I don't pay you enough for you to go spending large sums of money on gifts for me and Pearl. It was unnecessary.'

'I thought you liked it,' she said in dismay.

'Not enough to warrant that level of extravagance.'

'But you've bought me——'

'I happen to be a wealthy man,' he said, his handsome face cold. 'I can afford to indulge in mad whims like kitting out my child's governess for skiing, or buying her the odd gift. You can't. Don't do anything like that again.'

Dot took a deep breath, aware of coming down to earth rapidly. 'I won't,' she assured him.

'Christmas is for children. Now, shall we go to breakfast?'

A puzzled-looking Pearl brightened happily at their return. Calum, looking exactly as he always did, moved to serve up bacon and eggs while Oba-san supervised toast. Dot was wearing the pearls, but he didn't seem to notice.

'This is part of honourable Christmas routine in our country,' he explained drily to Oba-san. 'The men give presents, then the women run out of the room crying, and the bacon has to go black before they'll come back to eat it.' He gave Dot a cool look. 'Can we start now?'

'Of course,' said Dot, sitting opposite him. The Christmas festivities were now obviously over, and everything was getting back to normal.

Right from their arrival on the evening of Boxing Day, Hakuba was, against all odds, a dazzling success.

Hakuba's beauty quite bemused Dot. It was the kind of thing that could only happen in Japan—a Bavarian village, nestling in a fertile valley between peaks that were ten thousand miles from Bavaria.

The atmosphere was almost completely hybridised European, from the wooden buildings that belonged along the shores of some Austrian lake, to the restaurants and discos that would have been appropriate to Gstaad or Juan-les-Pins. Even the crowds who had come to ski weren't exclusively Japanese. Wherever they went, they heard German, French, Italian and English being spoken. The most Japanese aspect of the place was the cuisine. Though people danced to Munich oompah bands or British rock, they ate *tempura*, *soba*, *sukiyaki* and *chawanmushi*.

There was oceans of snow, piling up on the chalet-style roofs and in the cobbled streets, making the slopes paradise for the thousands of devotees who had arrived for Christmas.

The hotel would have earned its five stars anywhere in the world. It was frankly luxurious, and the room Dot had was a delight. The enormous double bed—a real live Western-style double bed!—was as soft as thistledown. The scale of the apartment was presidential. She had her own bathroom and shower, and a sitting-room equipped with TV, video and refrigerator, and her own balcony overlooking the snow-lined streets of Bavaria/Japan outside.

The details, like the beautiful sheets, and the huge, fluffy towels, were immaculate.

Even Calum and Pearl, sharing a similar room two floors below, hadn't done quite as well, in that their view wasn't as good.

'This is a *lovely* place,' Pearl had judged. Out of the way of sprung beds, she had to be restrained from using hers as a trampoline.

'It is lovely,' Dot said to Calum quietly. 'Thank you for bringing me here.'

'Please,' he had groaned, 'don't start being polite, after three months of open mutiny!'

There was no shortage of amusements for Pearl. The hotel contained a special lounge for children, in which Pearl swiftly found a host of friends of her own age, had a professionally run twenty-four-hour crèche, offered baby-sitters at any and every hour of the day or night, and ran its own junior skiing classes.

Pearl took to her lessons with her usual aplomb. Calum's prediction about her getting cold and wet was accurate, but after three days she was slithering down the nursery slopes with the best of them, delighting her instructor. The exhilaration on her round pink face was evident, and Dot felt she was watching the start of what would probably be a lifetime passion for Pearl. In a few years, she reflected wistfully, Pearl would be a lithe young beauty, hurtling down the perilous *pistes* of whatever country her father was currently living in, with an army of courting males in pursuit...

It was the perfect kind of holiday, geared for the adults as well as for the very young. A proliferation of entertainments was on offer. On New Year's Eve there was to be a children's party in the children's lounge, and a fancy-dress party for the adults in the hotel ballroom, a prospect which was making Dot rack her brains for a costume.

Like all Japanese resorts, Hakuba was crowded to capacity. This made the lower slopes something of a hazard, with first-time skiers careering helplessly in all directions, and it was only by taking the chair-lift to the higher slopes that it was possible to get areas of snow all to oneself.

Acting as Dot's part-time instructor, Calum had soon had her remembering all she had forgotten and learning a great deal more; and one afternoon they left Pearl in the hotel and took the chair-lift right up to Shohaku, one of the highest slopes, to get away from the crowds.

It was snowing lightly at the top, the powdery covering making for very fast, rather perilous skiing. The slopes looked almost vertical to Dot's wary eyes, and she was beginning to doubt the wisdom of having accepted Calum's challenge.

They got off at the final stop, and carried their skis to the edge of the slope.

'You have to watch the trees on this descent,' Calum was warning her. 'There's forest to your left all the way down, and there are a few big firs scattered along the *piste*. OK?'

'I'll just follow you,' Dot nodded. '*Please* don't go too fast.'

'I won't.' They stopped to get ready. Calum looked magnificent in dark blue, the close-fitting ski jacket emphasising the breadth of his shoulders and giving him a slightly military air. Idly, she watched snowflakes touching his tanned face, lasting a second before melting in his body heat. He knelt to check her ski-fastenings. 'How are you feeling in the joints department?' he asked, looking up.

'Sore,' she admitted, gathering her curly black hair into her cap. It had grown long and thick while she had been in Japan. 'My back, especially. I'm not used to the exercise, I guess.'

'No, it's sleeping in Western-style beds. I've been stiff too.'

'I must say that after longing for a sprung mattress for three months, I'm a little disappointed,' Dot smiled.

'Futons take a little getting used to, but they're good for sleeping on.'

'They're even better for making love on,' Calum said calmly, a sentiment which Dot wasn't qualified to comment on, and which effectively silenced her.

It was a long way to the bottom from this height. She pulled her hat well down and pulled the goggles over her eyes. The equipment Calum had bought her was superb, which gave her a little confidence for the descent ahead.

They waited for a party of students to set off ahead of them. The drifting snowflakes were not thick enough to limit visibility; they enhanced the beauty of the Alpine surroundings, lending mystery to the vast peaks all around. Dot was lost in the majesty of the setting for a while, just drinking it in, in a reverie which Calum did not disturb.

Then, with a gentle push of his ski-poles, he set off ahead of her, and she followed, bumping a little over unevennesses in the snow.

The descent was really a giant slalom, with trees and humps for obstacles, but at least there were few other skiers to contend with, and the woods and other dangers were well signposted with flags. He took the first two hundred yards nice and slowly, with gentle turns, and Dot had no trouble in keeping behind him.

On the next section, they picked up speed, Calum choosing a less oblique route down.

Dot started to feel the blood race in her veins, the exhilaration making her adrenalin flow. The silence was magical, only the hissing of their skis, and the occasional flurries of thrown-up snow, breaking the solitude.

To their left, the dark and shadowy woods sped by, and once a great white owl swooped out of the branches to cross their path. The turns were sharper now, and less rhythmical. Dot had to crouch lower, tucking the poles under her arms, feeling the muscles in her legs taking the strain.

It was beautiful, thrilling. Calum glanced over his shoulder at her from time to time to check that she was all right. They hurtled over a ridge, and on to a long, undulating field without obstacles, where they accelerated. The wind was whistling in Dot's ears, ruffling the collar of her jacket. Once she almost slipped on a tight turn, but her balance held good.

It was a long way down, though! After twenty minutes, her knees were starting to tremble, and her thighs and calves were aching. Speed and concentration had made her slightly dizzy. She didn't have either Calum's agility or his resilient muscles, but she was determined not to give way. She had been through so many ordeals for his sake, she wouldn't back out of this one now!

Without warning, however, her skis ploughed too deep into the snow on a turn, and her tired legs couldn't adjust. With a yelp, she was tumbling head over heels down a bank. She felt both skis come off her boots. The breath was momentarily knocked out of her lungs. She hadn't been going very fast, however, and the snow was soft, so it was mainly her dignity that had suffered.

Calum braked and plodded as fast as he could up the slope back to her, helping her to her feet and brushing snow off her. She pushed her goggles up into her hair and looked at him ruefully.

'Sorry,' she panted. 'My legs kind of died on me.'

'Are you hurt?'

'Only my pride.'

He looked relieved. 'We'll take a break,' he nodded. 'I'll find your skis—you get off the slope, or some *kamikaze* skier will run you over.'

Dot trudged towards the woods, thumping herself to get the rest of the snow off. She *would* have to take a tumble with Calum present! It was her fate. To put it in Japanese terms, her *karma* was perpetually to have honourable egg on face in front of Calum.

She had, at any rate, met her end in a magnificent spot. The view from here took in a range of peaks, shrouded in silent, misty grandeur, that would not have shamed the Swiss Alps. The firs were huge, towering overhead like mountain sentinels. Dot found a fallen log and sat on it, recovering her breath. Her knees were still quivering. The remainder of the descent would have to be at a snail's pace. Well, she tried to tell her injured self-respect, she hadn't done badly to get this far.

Calum approached, carrying her skis over his shoulder. She watched him warily. Perhaps for once he wasn't in the mood to heap coals of sarcasm on her head. In fact, his tanned face was split by a rare grin, showing his beautiful white teeth.

'You look a picture of dejection,' he said, pulling off his own skis and sitting beside her. 'Cheer up. You skied beautifully.'

'Did I?'

'Like a professional,' he assured her, his eyes glinting. He looked across the valley. 'You pick your places, anyway. Isn't that view incredible? Japan is so beautiful.'

'You're right, it is beautiful. I've grown to love it.'

She felt Calum's eyes on her. 'It shows.'

'Have I stopped making all those banal remarks?' she asked, meeting his gaze briefly.

'Almost,' he said with a half-smile. 'I'm glad you like the country. At first I thought you would never adjust. But you've adapted better than I ever expected you to. You've even picked up more than a smattering of Japanese.'

She gave him a mock-bow. *'Ah, so desu ka?'*

He smiled, and took from his pocket a bar of chocolate which they shared.

A group of skiers hissed past them, goggled faces intent as they weaved expertly down the slope. Seeing Calum glance at his watch, Dot gathered courage to tell him about her knees.

'They're very shaky. I practically wrecked one of them last time I skied, in Italy. I'll need a bit of a break before I can tackle the rest of it.'

Calum looked resigned. 'No hurry. Giggling knees have to be taken seriously.'

'Giggling knees?'

'That's the Japanese name for your condition.' He pulled off his gloves, made her sit facing him on the log, and lifted one of her legs on to his lap. Then, with strong, authoritative fingers, he started massaging her slender thigh.

The sensation of his thumbs ploughing over her trembling muscles was agitating at first, making her quiver in alarm; but after a short while the expert kneading became a warm pleasure that brought relief.

She watched his tanned hands moving rhythmically up and down her thigh. Such beautiful, strong hands. The right sort of hands for a man, precise and sexy. It was hard to remember that his touch was meant to be medicinal, not amorous.

'Any better?' he asked.

'Yes, much better. Is this some ancient Japanese art you've picked up from one of those young and beautiful geishas you were telling me about?'

'Nothing like that,' he said, deadpan. 'I've just been dying to squeeze your thighs all day.'

'Oh, what nonsense!' She flushed, feeling the sensuous power of his palms against her muscles.

'Why should it be nonsense? They're beautiful thighs.'

'Not in these ski-pants.'

'I've seen them out of their ski-pants,' he reminded her huskily.

Whatever it was doing for her giggling knees, his touch was starting to affect her in a quite different way.

'Well, beautiful thighs or not, do you still want to see them walking back to England?' Dot asked him, meeting his eyes briefly.

He motioned for her other leg before replying.

'If I said I was starting to appreciate you a lot more,' he said quietly, resuming his massage, 'you'd probably misunderstand me. You're apt to get big-headed.'

'Am I?'

'Definitely. You need keeping in order.' His hands spread warmth up her thigh. 'You've done wonders for Pearl, and I don't know how I would ever have coped without you. You've taught her to read, for which I'll be grateful to you all my life.'

'Gratitude *and* praise,' she said drily. 'I must be dreaming!'

Calum's mouth was ironic. 'See what I mean? It goes straight to your head.'

'Well, when I first arrived,' Dot reminded him, trying to keep her mind off what his hands were doing to her, 'you refused to believe that I could have any good effect on Pearl at all. You seemed to think I was here to poison her mind against you. I think you still believe that, deep inside.'

'Don't be absurd!'

'Absurd? Have you forgotten what you were doing to me in the squash court last week?'

'You said you enjoyed the game,' Calum replied innocently.

'Do people usually enjoy being pulverised? Have you *any* idea how utterly foully you've treated me for the past three months? How rude you've been, how many humiliating situations you've put me in, how many cruel things you've said and done to me?'

The glint in his deep eyes showed amusement, rather than remorse. 'What have you stuck around for, then?' he asked.

'Goodness knows,' she retorted. 'Partly for your daughter's sake, and partly just to spite you.'

'And what did you think you'd achieve by spiting me?' Calum enquired, lifting one eyebrow at her.

'Well, it helped me preserve my self-respect, at least. Why are you always so down on me?'

'Because you're a disruption,' he said flatly. 'You always will be.' His strong, warm hands were massaging rather higher up her thigh than was necessary, making her breath come quicker.

'What kind—of disruption?' she asked, forcing herself to keep her voice normal.

'You make the whole situation a lot more difficult than it needs to be.'

'Difficult in what way?'

'Supposing a tender, juicy young gazelle was put into a tiger's cave, to care for little Miss Cub while Mrs Tiger was out with the girls. Wouldn't that make life rather difficult for Mr Tiger?'

'But that's Mr Tiger's problem,' said Dot. 'It doesn't help to take it out on the poor gazelle!'

'I've been finding that out,' Calum agreed, concentrating on his task. 'But Mr Tiger has to take the steps he thinks most appropriate.'

'Like growling and snarling from morning till midnight?'

'Frustrated tigers get ill-tempered.'

Didn't he notice what his hands were doing? He was caressing her in a way that was just short of erotic, his kneading fingers spreading a languorous warmth through her lower body.

'I don't see why you should be frustrated.'

His eyes were dark blue pools. 'Don't you?'

'Well, I realise that you're a free man,' Dot said boldly. 'But I'm not exactly a rose without thorns—you said so. You also said you prefer your women experienced.'

'I do.'

'Well then? You can't possibly complain that I inflame your passions. With all those highly trained geishas in Tokyo, how can you say you're frustrated? You could go to some pretty young thing who has six degrees in pacifying tigers—*Calum*!'

His hand had roamed so far between her legs that she broke off on a gasp, and trapped it with her fingers, stopping the voluptuous ordeal he was subjecting her to.

'My knees have stopped giggling now,' she said in a strained voice.

'Yes, but has your mouth stopped moving?' he asked menacingly.

'Yes!'

'Glad to hear it,' he said equably. A glance at her flushed cheeks would have told him just what she was feeling. Dot released his trapped hand and swung her legs over the log to prevent any future peril. Nerves in her stomach were still quivering from his touch. 'You still haven't answered my question,' she challenged. 'Are you going to send me back or not?'

'Well,' he countered, looking into her eyes, 'you said yourself that you thought it would be the best idea, before we left Chinsanzo. Is that what you want?'

'I don't think it would be the best thing for Pearl,' she said quietly. 'But it might be the best thing for us.'

'Us?' echoed Calum with a touch of mockery.

'For me, then,' she said in an even lower voice. 'I hate to feel that I'm the cause of discord between you and Pearl. That isn't what I want.'

'And what *do* you want?' he asked in a velvety voice.

'I'll go along with whatever arrangement you have in mind,' Dot said, not meeting his eyes.

'The kind of arrangements I have in mind are evidently not to your taste.'

'What does that mean?' she asked, grey eyes widening.

'You obviously find me repulsive,' he said evenly, 'or you wouldn't scream for help every time I come near you. So I keep growling and snarling. Ready to go?'

In truth, she was feeling a lot weaker and wobblier now than when he had started on her, but she could hardly tell him that.

She buckled on her skis in silence, her muscles feeling about as strong as wet brown paper. She cursed the desire he had awakened in her. It had been deliberate, she was sure; he knew a great deal more about her erogenous zones than she liked.

It had stunned her that he had finally admitted that the real problem lay with *his* feelings about her, rather than with her relationship with Pearl.

But what had he meant by that last crack? Was that little parable about the tiger and the gazelle an invitation to have an affair with him?

Did he really think *that* would solve their problems?

She had to shelve all mental baggage to concentrate on the helter-skelter downward run. Calum made the concession of taking the rest of the descent at an almost moderate pace, and though Dot had several close shaves she didn't actually fall again until they were right down at the village. By then she was as weak as a kitten, and had to endure Calum's amusement as he practically carried her to a bar for a restorative rum and coffee.

The three days leading up to New Year's Eve passed swiftly.

Skiing or sightseeing in the beautiful mountain scenery took up their mornings and afternoons; their nights were filled with music and company. An integral ingredient of the fun of Hakuba was the vibrant *après-ski* scene. There was the most tempting shopping Dot had seen outside Tokyo, and night life to rival any Alpine resort, both in Hakuba itself and in the pretty little town of Tsugaike nearby, which boasted dozens of discos and eating places.

Calum had many friends here; wherever he and Dot went, he was recognised by people eager to renew the acquaintance, and they were never short of company of various nationalities. The number of people who assumed they were married, and that the dark-haired Pearl was Dot's daughter, was at first embarrassing, then amusing.

It didn't matter. They were simply having fun, in the company of young people of every nationality. It was a bubbling, international atmosphere, testifying to the excellence of the Japanese slopes and the glittering amusements on offer.

Nor did they have to worry about Pearl if they wanted to spend an afternoon or an evening together. The hotel staff took care of everything. The crèche, or a baby-sitter provided by the hotel, meant that Calum had been able to take Dot to dine out and dance the night away every evening since they had arrived.

There was a new mood between her and Calum. The months of hostility between them had not been completely forgotten; but it was as though the cause of tension between them had suddenly started to be exciting rather than upsetting.

When they bickered now, as they did constantly, it always ended in laughter. It had become almost a game between them, a kind of sparkling truce among the snowy beauties of Hakuba.

They were becoming a couple. It occurred to Dot that it was more like being on a honeymoon than a holiday.

The biggest worry on her mind was what to wear for the fancy dress party; but inspiration dawned with a day to spare.

She would go as a geisha. A young and beautiful one, naturally!

Though she had got used to wearing kimonos, she had never really tried out the full classical outfit worn by traditional Japanese women. She had been put off by the elaborate and, to her mind, tedious details. Hanako, she knew, needed twenty full minutes to dress, and her clothes were relatively informal. Geishas were encased in up to six layers of clothing, involving padding, stiffening, sashes, straps, pins, clips, combs, and more than a dozen different garments. But the idea was such fun, and would amuse Calum so much, that her heart was set on it.

Her eye had been caught by a particularly beautiful shop in one of the main streets, selling classical Japanese wear for women. She knew it would be an expensive exercise, but she had spent practically nothing since coming to Japan, apart from the bonsai tree for Calum, and it wasn't as though she was short of money.

She slipped out of the hotel, walked to the shop through the snowy streets, and entered a scented, rustling world of silks and sashes. Her Japanese was by now good enough to explain what she wanted without once resorting to English. The diminutive proprietress and her assistants were at first sceptical about her height, then entered into the spirit of the thing with delight.

Choosing the clothes was almost as much fun as being shown how to put them on. Dot soon realised that she would have to get help from the hotel staff to dress and do her hair on the night. She would never manage on her own. But that wouldn't be a problem, and the clothes were so beautiful that she knew they would always be an enchanting souvenir of one of the happiest weeks of her life.

The giggling attendants presented her, as a gift, with a case of ornamental combs and pins, and a beautifully painted parasol to complete the outfit. She checked herself in the mirror and knew the outfit was right. Delighted with her purchases, Dot changed, paid, and made her way happily back to her room.

CHAPTER EIGHT

DOT came down from her room, wrapped in the emerald silk *obi*, and tapped on Calum's door. Pearl opened it, gasping with awe as she walked in. Calum stood as if rooted to the spot.

The look on his face when he first saw her would stay with Dot for ever.

She had fought shy of the white mask of make-up that a true geisha would have worn—that only suited Japanese faces. So she had just emphasised her full lips with a scarlet lipstick instead, and had allowed herself a free hand with the mascara and eye-shadow. A fancy dress party was one occasion when you could let yourself go!

Calum walked round her slowly, taking her in with those wonderful dark eyes. 'Where on earth did you get that costume?' he asked at last.

She told him. 'Do you like it?' she asked anxiously, just in case she had misread the expression on his face.

'You're exquisite,' he said simply, his voice husky. 'There aren't other words.' He touched the gleaming swathe of her black hair, secured by the hotel hairdresser into an elaborate chignon that left her slender neck free. 'And you smell of...'

'Apricots,' she supplied, made shy by the look in his eyes. She twirled her parasol. 'They said it was an authentic geisha scent. Is it?'

'I've never noticed.' He touched his lips to her neck, inhaling her scent. 'It's delicious.' He trailed long, lean fingers across the silk sash around her middle, and shook his head in wonder. 'I never dreamed...' He didn't finish the sentence. 'Well,' he smiled instead, 'you and I couldn't have made a greater contrast. Talk about Beauty and the Beast!'

His costume was, indeed, very different from hers. Wearing tight denims, heavy boots and a leather jacket covered with metal studs and crossed with a chrome chain, he was unmistakably the barbaric leader of a motorcycle gang. He had completed the picture with sinister wrap-around sunglasses and a heavy steel bracelet around each muscular wrist. He could have stepped out of the set of *The Wild Ones* or *Easy Rider*.

'Where did *you* get *that* outfit?' she countered.

'Various shops,' he grinned. 'The sunglasses and manacles came from a disreputable friend, and there's even a motorbike outside if you want the full realism. The nose,' he added drily, 'I supplied myself.'

'How *did* you get that nose?' Dot wanted to know. 'I've been dying to ask.'

'Squash,' he said succinctly. 'Sorry it's so prosaic. It ought to have been done by a rival lover, but in fact someone took too much of a swing with his racket, and I woke up with this conk.'

'Damn!' said Dot, wide-eyed. 'I knew there was something I was missing that day. I'll remember next time we play.'

'Just try it,' he growled.

The effect, she thought, was all too vivid. With that ruthlessly male face and that muscular body he was almost frightening. The crooked nose might have been the souvenir of some savage brawl, and the glinting blue eyes hinted at a nature capable of anything...

It was almost a relief to see him scoop Pearl up in his arms and give her a cuddle. She was squealing with delight at the transformation that had overtaken the two most important people in her life.

'Why can't I dress up too?' she demanded, fascinated by Dot's ornate costume.

'Because you're going to your own party,' Calum smiled. 'You like balloons, toys, games, puzzles, chocolate cake, ice-cream and lemonade, don't you?'

'Yes!'

'Well, there won't be any of those lovely things where Dot and I are going. Only champagne and smoked salmon and caviar—things that you hate.'

'Oh!' Pearl's disappointment melted in her pity at the dull time Dot and her father were going to have, and she went off to her party quite cheerfully.

Dot and Calum's evening was wonderful, right from the start. She had known it was going to be special, the happiest night of her life.

Her geisha outfit was a stunning success. Though not suitable for any dance less decorous than a waltz, it attracted universal admiration in the crowded ballroom, and more than one pair of male eyes were transfixed on her.

'Will you stop making eyes at all these men!' Calum growled fiercely, whirling her on to the dance floor.

'I wasn't,' she protested. 'I only have eyes for you...Marlon Brando.'

'Where do I hold you?' he puzzled, looking at her silky outline. 'I don't want to crease that beautiful *obi*.'

Dot produced a scarlet fan from her sash and fluttered her mascaraed lashes at him over it. 'Honourable *obi* made to be creased,' she cooed.

Calum grinned, his eyes dancing. 'I'd better keep a tight hold of you, then.'

'Welcome, but why?'

He smiled down at her. 'Oh, geishas are notoriously flighty. Japanese poetry is full of sad tales about *samurais* who had the misfortune to fall in love with one. As soon as a richer master came along, she would spread her bright wings and be gone. Even in the middle of a crowd, like this.'

'Not this geisha,' said Dot, folding her fan with a click. 'This geisha has been paid for *all* night.'

The emphasis she put on the word 'all' made him look swiftly into her eyes. Did he see the promise in them? Did he know that tonight she was his, that she was not going to scream for help?

He lifted one of her slender hands to his mouth and kissed it gently. 'We have tonight, then,' he said softly, 'before you fly away. Let's dance, Madam Butterfly.'

The hours passed in dancing, eating and drinking. Dot felt as though she were floating on bright clouds. She was in the company of the man who meant more to her than any other, dancing on top of the world...

They looked in on Pearl twice, the second time to take a very sleepy little girl to bed.

Calum watched while Dot tucked the child up.

'Happy New Year, little one,' Dot whispered, kissing the smooth cheek.

She put out the light, and they returned to the whirl and the noise.

As the hour approached midnight, their conversation turned inevitably to the future.

'What are you going to do when your contract expires?' Dot ventured, sipping champagne during a break in the dancing. 'Will you stay on in Japan?'

'I'm very tempted,' Calum nodded. 'The corporation want me to sign up for a five-year spell, principally to supervise the new generation of computers they're bringing out.'

'And is that what you want?'

'I don't know,' he said frankly. 'I've had another offer which I might not be able to refuse.'

'From a rival company?'

'From the University of California, in Los Angeles. To take up the Chair of Computer Technology there.'

'A professorship?' Dot asked in awe. 'Wow!'

'Yes.' He grimaced. 'I don't know whether the academic life would really suit me. Professor Hescott? How does that sound?'

'It sounds wonderful to me,' said Dot—then regretted her breathless tone as she caught his ironic look. She lightened her voice. 'Well, in that outfit, maybe not. They wouldn't let you into the faculty with that steel chain on!'

'Have you seen American academics?' he grinned.

'I suppose it would mean a very different kind of life,' she mused, lifting a sliver of smoked salmon to her painted lips.

Calum nodded. 'It would mean taking a cut in salary, for one thing. Five more years in Japan would make me very rich. But I don't need the money, Dot. Not any more. I've taken out patents on some of my developments, and the way things are going, they'll bring in a great deal of money over the next few years. A life income, in fact.' He glanced at her. 'Have you ever been to California?'

'I've never been to America at all,' she said wistfully.

'It's very different from this. Or England.'

She followed the dancing, her clear grey eyes misty with thought. 'Would you regret leaving Japan?'

'Well, I love the States. Especially California. And Silicon Valley is where everything is happening in my field. But yes,' Calum sighed, 'I'm very torn. My work here is fascinating, for one thing. As a university professor, I'd be engaged in very theoretical work, and I don't know whether I would adjust. I also enjoy the Japanese way of life for another thing. It's very tranquil, and I've grown to appreciate tranquillity. California is very laid back by American standards, but life there is hardly lying under palm trees, eating oranges all day.'

'It always looks like a sort of earthly paradise to me,' Dot confessed. 'It has a wonderful climate, hasn't it?'

'Also earthquakes, smog and crime,' he said drily. He tapped the chrome chain. 'I might have to wear this to get into work in the mornings.'

'You can have earthquakes and smog here,' Dot pointed out, watching his crooked-nosed profile, 'if not so much crime. But five years is a long time. For Pearl, I mean.'

'Yes,' Calum nodded, 'Pearl is one of the main problems. There are English-language schools in Tokyo, but she'd be very much cut off from the West here.' He looked at Dot with a half-smile. 'One thing you've shown me is that Pearl needs to grow up in a culture that's her own, that she has a right to. America is a lot closer to home than Japan, if I can put it that way.'

'When do you have to give an answer?'

'I have to make my mind up in a few weeks, no more.'

They sat in silence. Dot was lost in sad thoughts. His life was so different from hers. His horizons lay beyond her line of vision. Whatever happened, her time with him was strictly limited. Even if he didn't send her back now, in six months' time her present contract would be over. She couldn't spend the next five years as a governess in Japan if Calum decided to stay in Tokyo. And she couldn't follow him to America if he decided to take up the professorship. Soon, very soon, this part of her life would be over.

And then she would be going back to England to look for another job. Another family, another spell working in someone else's home, with someone else's children...

She thought of those grim-faced, spinsterish governesses sitting in Michael Osborne's office that day. Would she suddenly find one day that she was middle-aged and alone, that life had passed her by?

The thought was infinitely depressing. She didn't want to go back to England. She didn't want to leave Pearl.

Why not admit the truth? She didn't want to leave Calum.

She must be some sort of masochist, Dot thought glumly, to want to stick with someone who treated her the way Calum did. But he was under her skin, in her system, deep within her heart. She was permeated by him to the extent that she just couldn't see a life without him.

Suddenly, tonight with Calum was very precious...

As though picking up her thoughts, he smiled. 'Only twenty more minutes of the old year left. Will you dance with me?'

'There's no one I'd rather dance with.'

Twenty minutes glided swiftly away in his arms, the cacophony of voices, music and laughter building up in a wave of excitement towards midnight. There was room for just a few thoughts of sadness at the parting of the year, of those who were not here. The tears started to her eyes, but Calum must have understood, because he just held her close, and let her gulp away the sadness.

Then the countdown to midnight had started. Calum grinned at her as the crowd took up the chant.

'Have you made a resolution yet?' he asked.

Dot shook her head dumbly, lost in her feelings for this man she had travelled ten thousand miles to find, this person she hadn't dreamed of twelve months ago, who was now the centre of her universe.

An explosion of frantic noise ended the countdown. It was midnight. One year had passed, and another had begun.

Calum simply reached for her, his mouth hungering for hers.

Her eyes were tight shut, and she was clinging to Calum as he kissed her mouth, her mind flooded with emotion. They stood locked together among the cascading balloons and whirling streamers, intent only on one another...

Slowly, reluctantly, they parted, Dot looking up at him with dazed eyes, her lips bruised by his kiss.

'Happy New Year, Dot,' he said huskily.

'Happy New Year,' she whispered, her words lost among the noise.

'Shall we be alone?' he asked, his mouth close to her ear, 'just you and I?'

'Yes!'

They pushed through the streamer-throwing, whooping, champagne-drinking crowds, shaking hands and bestowing or receiving kisses on all sides. It took them ten minutes to get out, and once outside Calum took her in his arms and kissed her again, his mouth fierce and possessive.

Dot's heart was pounding in her throat. 'Not here,' she whimpered, shaking her head. 'Let's go to my room.'

He smiled wickedly. 'Some virgin!'

'Not tonight,' she said, her cheeks colouring.

His expression changed.

'Come on, then,' he commanded, leading her to the lift.

They let themselves into Dot's room, the silence deafening after the noise downstairs. She felt very strange,

emotional and yet excited to the core. She switched on
the soft light of a bedside lamp, then turned to face him,
suddenly overcome with shyness.

'Do you want a drink?' she asked, dry-mouthed, '...or
anything?'

'I'll settle for getting out of this ridiculous get-up first,'
he smiled, his eyes smoky. 'And then the anything.'

He hauled off the leather jacket and the T-shirt and
sat on a chair, bare-chested, to take off the boots. Dot
watched the muscles of his shoulders ripple, her pulses
starting to pound. Then he was stepping out of his jeans,
and wearing only a pair of very brief black briefs he
came towards her.

He was so beautiful. As he took her in his arms, his
body was taut with the promise of desire. She melted
against him with a little gasp, her lips parting as he possessed them. Her hands trembled as they touched him,
caressed the skin that was like hot velvet against her.

'Oh,' he whispered raggedly, 'I want you so much,
Dot. I've wanted you for months...' He looked frus-
tratedly at her outfit. 'How the hell do I get you out of
all that silk?'

'I thought you'd know,' she laughed shakily. 'You're
the expert on geishas.'

'I've never been to one in my life,' he said with a wry
smile. 'Not the kind you mean.'

Dot stared at him. 'You're teasing me!'

'I'm not.'

'But all those nights you were out?'

'Dorothy.' He cupped her oval face in his hands, and
looked into her eyes. 'I just got drunk with the rest of
them, trying to forget the way I felt about you. I haven't
had a woman in three months. Not since you came.'

'Oh, Calum...'

'Since the day I saw you, standing sweetly naked by the pool, I haven't wanted another woman. I've only wanted you. Did I say wanted?' He laughed huskily. 'I mean craved for you. Ached for you, died for you...'

His words were making her dizzy. 'I can't believe it,' she whispered.

'Why do you think I've had to be so brutal with you?' He kissed her mouth, hard. 'To stop myself from ravishing you, from starting a wild affair with my child's governess. I'm crazy about you, Dorothy. Don't you know that by now?'

Dot's knees were weak. She sank down among the piled-up pillows, looking up at him with drowned eyes. 'And I've been your slave for months,' she said unsteadily. 'Don't you know that?'

He sank down beside her. 'Give me a clue,' he said in a tight voice, taking a fold of the emerald silk in his hand. 'Where do I start?'

'Here,' she whispered, and reached up to take the comb out of her hair. The dark, fragrant curls escaped, dropping to frame her flushed face. 'And here.' She kicked off the white silk slippers. 'Can you work out the rest?'

Calum kissed her clinging lips, laughing softly. 'Who'd have thought you'd turn out such a wanton?' He reached for the knot of her sash. 'This must be the way in,' he decided, tugging the bow loose.

Dot lay back, looking into his face with a soft smile. 'Have you overcome your scruples about having an affair with your child's governess yet?'

'Not really.' He drew the long sash away from her waist and let it flutter brightly to the carpet. His fingers eased the emerald-green *obi* away from her shoulders. 'But I've reached a conclusion that will answer admirably.'

'Tell me about it,' she invited.

'What, right now?'

'There's plenty of time,' Dot said mischievously. 'You've got a long way to go.'

'So I see,' he said, his expression amused. Underneath the green *obi* was another, of lemon-yellow silk, secured by another sash. His warmly amused eyes met hers. 'How long did it take you to get all these esoteric garments on?'

'Half an hour,' she said smugly. 'But then I had help.'

'I see.' He unfastened the second sash, unwinding it from her waist with sensual care. 'Well,' he purred, 'I have a new arrangement in mind. First of all, I sack you,'

'Sack me?' Dot exclaimed, sitting up with bright eyes. 'Of all the ungrateful, low-down tricks——'

'Oh, I'm a pig, underlined twice. But surely you've realised that by now?' He pushed her firmly back against the pillows and kissed her throat with warm lips.

She cradled his head, her fingers roaming through his crisp, clean hair. 'How can you possibly sack me?' she moaned.

'Easily. I've been waiting three months for the right opportunity.' He was leaning over her, his hands moving at the small of her back. 'There's a sort of cushion thing in here.'

'To keep the bow up,' she explained. 'And to give one a nice bottom.'

'You've already got a nice bottom,' he said appreciatively, discarding the cushion.

'So they told me at the shop,' Dot said gently. 'But I wanted to get the details right.'

His fingers explored gently. 'And this silver thing?'

'A pin to keep the cushion in place.' Her hands were linked round Calum's muscular neck as he undressed her. 'Careful,' she warned, 'it's sharp!'

'I'm glad you told me. You could do an unwary *samurai* a nasty injury with this.' He laid the pin and the cushion on the bedside table and considered her. She was still very far from undressed, but there was more of her on show now. He kissed her lips, his mouth demanding and yet giving, his tongue probing her response.

'That scent suits you,' he whispered. 'I want you always to wear it when we come to bed.'

His lips caressed her eyelids teasingly, moving to her temples, her cheeks, the sensitive shells of her ears. She arched to him, whimpering. What was she to do? He had said he preferred his women experienced; was she being painfully gauche and shy? She, at least, didn't have the obstacles of clothing. Her timid hands reached for him, seeking and caressing. She had longed to touch him for so long, to lay her palm over his heart and feel the engine pounding under the firm, warm flesh, to run her fingers down his flanks, feeling the hard ribs tapering down to his lithe waist, reaching the line of his briefs.

Gently, shyly, her fingers traced the elastic inwards along his belly, following the swelling triangle of black cotton that was stretched taut over the hot centre of his manhood.

Her touch was so delicate that he could hardly have felt it, and yet it made him groan with pleasure, encouraging her to be bolder, her palm brushing the arrogant fullness that was so strange and yet so exciting to her.

His face was flushed with passion as he whispered her name, her shyly exploring touch seeming to madden him. He pulled apart the second *obi*.

'Now what?' he groaned, reaching the flat, linen-covered board over her stomach.

'Take it away,' whispered Dot. 'It's just there to make the *obi* look neat.'

He lifted it out, putting it with the cushion and the pin. Frustration was making both of them pant now, their desire mounting to a furnace heat.

'You were saying something—something about dismissing me,' Dot said unevenly.

'Ah, yes. Now I've sacked you,' he went on, helping her out of the *obi*, 'you're no longer my daughter's governess. Do you see the brilliance of it? All my moral scruples now fall aside.'

'But supposing *my* moral scruples don't fall aside so easily?' Dot suggested. She was wearing only her silk briefs and a little linen jacket now, and her breath was coming fast and shallow.

'Oh, I've thought of a solution to that problem too.' He touched the linen jacket. 'What's under this?'

'Me,' she said.

'Ah!' His eyes glittered as he started to unfasten the tiny ribbons that held it together.

'What's your solution?' asked Dot in a barely audible voice.

'It's very simple.' At last the jacket was unfastened and he slid it off, his eyes dropping to her small, neat breasts, the nipples jutting tightly in a way that reflected her desire. The pearls he had given her were round her throat, glowing against the silky skin between her breasts. 'Very simple,' he repeated, more huskily. 'I ask you to marry me.'

Dot felt her heart flip over inside her. Disbelief made her lips part silently for a moment. '*Marry* you?' she echoed.

'Become my wife.' He saw her dazed expression. 'Plight our troth,' he said drily. 'Tie the knot. Become one flesh. Mr and Mrs. Have more children, start a life together. Is that such a terrible fate?'

'It's more than I ever dreamed,' she whispered, her eyes filling with tears. 'Oh, Calum, do you mean it?'

'I can't live without you,' he said gently, taking her in his arms. 'I love you, Dorothy. Will you marry me?'

'Of course I'll marry you,' she said, half laughing, half crying. 'I love you with every fibre of my heart!'

'I never thought you'd say yes,' he said, looking dazed. 'I thought you detested me, found me repulsive...'

'Repulsive!'

'Well, when I read that letter you wrote Barbara, I was plunged into despair. You seemed to hate me so—so *vehemently*.'

'But you were treating me so cruelly at that time,' she said, wiping the tears from her long lashes. 'I still don't think you know how frightening you were!'

'Well, you made me so angry.'

'How?'

'You were so cool, so touch-me-not.' He traced the pink peaks of her nipples with his fingertips, making her sigh voluptuously. 'Once I'd seen this marvellous body, I couldn't get it out of my thoughts. I saw it in my dreams, whenever I shut my eyes. I was like that bad monk, carrying a girl in my thoughts all day long. It was driving me mad!'

'Hey!' she said as his palms brushed her breasts.

'Hey what?'

'Hey, don't stop,' she commanded, and moaned softly as he cupped the firm, uptilted curves in his palms. 'And don't stop talking either!'

'I've been obsessed by you, my love—haunted, addicted. You accused me of being jealous of you. You couldn't have been more wrong. It was Pearl I was jealous of.'

'Pearl?' she echoed.

'Yes, Pearl, my own daughter.' His brows descended. 'She was all you seemed to be interested in, all you cared about. Any time I tried to talk to you, you'd only talk about Pearl. Pearl's needs, and Pearl's education, and what was best for Pearl. I could have throttled you at times! You never seemed to care about *my* needs. You were such a—such a *governess*!'

'Oh, Calum, how could you have been so blind? Didn't you see that I adored you? Couldn't you tell that I was only waiting for a gentle word from you, or a gentle touch, to stop being a governess and melt all over you, the way I was aching to do?'

His eyes were dark. 'I only saw that whenever I tried to make love to you, you rejected me.'

'I'm not rejecting you now,' she said softly.

He didn't answer. His mouth was tracing a line of kisses down the valley between her breasts, over the silky plane of her stomach.

She lay, trembling, and let him love her, the way he wanted to.

Her man was a magnificent lover, his touch was so sure, the pleasure he brought her so dizzyingly intense. Her fears and reservations were irrelevant. Long before he possessed her as a woman he had shown her what miracles lay in her body, unsuspected for twenty-five years. Sex was something she had read about, dreamed about. But she had never guessed that it could be this beauty, this flame that enveloped them and burned around them. She had known, in an abstract way, that men and women did these things. But the reality was so warm, so loving and so logical, that there could be neither shyness nor fear.

And when at last he came to her, his lovemaking was overwhelmingly tender. The searing moment in which she became his was brief, the pain fading into a flood of sweetness that filled her whole body, as high tide floods a beach, resolving into a rhythm that took her beyond the present, into a high, boundless place where there were no walls, no sky, no stars, only the two of them, their souls and their bodies fused into one ecstatic being...

The climax of their lovemaking was an irresistible force, driving them together. Mouth on mouth, thigh on thigh, bodies and minds locked in a shuddering culmination that rocked the world, they embraced, cried out each other's names, kissed each other's mouths and faces...

Reality was a long time coming back. Dot was pillowed on his broad chest, his hands caressing her tumbled hair.

'Calum,' she whispered.

'I'm here.'

'I love you so much...'

'I love you, Dot.'

'Do you still want to marry me?'

Calum laughed softly. 'I still want to marry you. Now go to sleep.'

She let dreams overwhelm her, secure in her love.

September in California was a warm, generous month. Fruit was heavy in the trees, and a sweet-scented flower was making the whole state giddy with perfume.

The windows of the faculty common-room had been thrown open to the balmy evening, and Dot welcomed the cool breeze that drifted in from the fountain across her tanned skin.

'Your daughter's a real charmer, Mrs Hescott,' the tall woman in the caftan was saying. 'Such a pretty, bright little girl, and so like you.'

'You're very kind.' Dot found no difficulty in hiding her smile. She didn't bother to correct people any more. After all, the little girl who now called her 'Mama' was as much hers, and she was as much her mother, as law and love could make them.

'Don't let her lose that beautiful English accent,' the tall woman's husband was saying. 'I just hope it'll rub off on our children. Do you think she'll settle to California?'

'Pearl's going to love it here,' said Dot, with complete certainty. 'This must be one of the best places in the world for children to grow up in.'

'I guess it's very different from Japan,' the man smiled. 'I can't tell you how proud and pleased we all are that your husband has come to join us. His presence makes this the foremost teaching and research school in the world.'

'Well, I know that Calum's proud and pleased to be here. We're both so excited and happy about being at UCLA.'

The three of them glanced across to where Calum was in conversation with two other professors, his handsome face alight with intelligence and life.

Her husband.

It still made her heart flip over inside her to realise that that tall, magnificent man was her husband. Her partner for life, her burning lover of the night-time, her joyous companion of the days...

'How old is she?' the tall woman's husband was asking.

'Pearl?' Dot returned to reality. 'She's five. She turned five in Barbados, a month ago.'

'Barbados,' the woman said enviously. 'A holiday?'

'No. Our honeymoon.'

Both of her companions nodded, smiling. Then the smiles did a double-take as the couple registered what Dot had said.

'Your *honeymoon*?'

Mischievous laughter bubbled up inside Dot at their expressions.

'We were married in London. We have a very dear aunt there, you see. And then we spent a month in the Caribbean, on a yacht, before coming here.'

'How lovely.' The tall woman was obviously bursting to ask why they had waited until their daughter was five years old before getting married, but was far too polite to do so.

Dot decided to put them out of their misery, but before she could explain about Pearl, Calum was heading her way, carrying a plate. His eyes were warm with love as they met hers.

'Here,' he said, 'I've managed to find some.'

'Gherkins!' Dot exclaimed in delight. She gave him a grateful kiss, and tucked into the plate ravenously.

The tall woman and her husband were by now watching in a stunned silence as Dot disposed of the crunchy little green things like someone who hadn't eaten since yesterday.

'She gets these cravings,' Calum explained apologetically. 'Yesterday it was ice-cream. I had to rush out and buy a scoop of chocolate and vanilla, and by the time I got back to the house, she was lying in the pool, saying she'd changed her mind and wanted pickled onions instead.'

'It's usually sour things,' smiled Dot. 'But sometimes it's something sweet instead.'

Their eyes were locked together, their secret smiles communicating the complete confidence of deep and unquestioned love between a man and a woman.

'So,' the tall woman said hesitantly, 'am I right, Mrs Hescott, in assuming—you're expecting?'

'Next February,' Dot nodded, finishing off the gherkins regretfully, and feeling slightly vinegary for a moment.

'Well, well!' The tall woman's husband was grinning widely. 'We're getting four for the price of three.' He lifted his glass of champagne in a toast to them. 'Here's to your second child, Mrs Hescott!'

'Er—not exactly.'

'I'm sorry?'

'This will be my first child,' explained Dot, poker-faced. 'I'm looking forward to it so much.'

The expressions were frozen for a second time, and Calum had to intervene with an explanation that had everyone laughing with the relief of the ex-bewildered.

'You're going to have to stop doing that to people,' he murmured in her ear as he ushered her away. 'It's a mean trick.'

'But they always jump to conclusions,' she smiled. 'Anyway, they're going to be our friends, so they might as well get used to our somewhat unconventional family set-up.'

They went out on to the balcony, arm in arm, and looked out over the beautiful garden of palm trees and oleanders, listening to the tinkle of the fountain. Behind them, the chatter of the party went on unabated.

'This is beautiful. What a place to work in!' sighed Calum. 'We're going to be so happy here.'

'Yes. We're going to be fulfilled, and happy, and utterly saturated in love...'

His fingers were tight around hers. 'Are you serious about taking this degree in computer science?'

'I've got a lifetime of Professor Hescott ahead of me, so I might as well find out what exactly it is you do for a living. Who knows? I might even get a job building ETRON III, one day. I'm not just a pretty face, you know. And since you've stopped paying me my salary...'

'Mercenary minx! But how will I ever manage to concentrate on teaching, with you sitting in the front row, smiling at me with that gorgeous, soft mouth?'

'You'll have to exercise some self-control,' Dot said, giving him exactly the kind of smile she knew most made his blood start to race. 'Have I really got a gorgeous, soft mouth?'

'You've got everything,' he assured her softly, 'that I'll ever want.'

'Even with all these pretty young students milling round you, with their blonde hair and heaving bosoms?'

'You've got a head start, my darling. You know the secrets of the Orient.'

'Ah. I'd forgotten.' She reached up and laid her hand on his broad chest. 'Calum...'

'Not more gherkins!' he groaned, misreading her expression.

'No. Do you think it's being pregnant that makes me come over all lustful about you?'

'Stop it!' he muttered, his eyes glittering. 'People will hear you!'

'I'll whisper, then,' she said, with a saintly expression. 'When we get home after this party, I'm going to...'

His eyes widened as he listened, and when she had finished, he looked down at her with a smoky expression that told her that he was now feeling exactly as desirous and lascivious as she was.

'And how am I supposed to go back in there and be the ascetic professor now?' he demanded huskily.

'You'll have to try, my darling,' she said innocently. 'Just remember that I love you, and you'll manage.'

'I love you too,' he said with a smile. 'But I should never have married a geisha...'

He kissed her gorgeous, soft mouth, then led her back to the party.

HARLEQUIN
Romance

Coming Next Month

Available in August wherever paperback books are sold, or through Harlequin Reader Service:

In the U.S.
901 Fuhrmann Blvd.
P.O. Box 1397
Buffalo, N.Y. 14240-1397

In Canada
P.O. Box 603
Fort Erie, Ontario
L2A 5X3

COMING SOON

DREAMSCAPE
Harlequin.
ROMANCE ™

In August, two worlds will collide in four very special romance titles. Somewhere between first meeting and happy ending, Dreamscape Romance will sweep you to the very edge of reality where everyday reason cannot conquer unlimited imagination—or the power of love. The timeless mysteries of reincarnation, telepathy, psychic visions and earthbound spirits intensify the modern lives and passion of ordinary men and women with an extraordinary alluring force.

Available next month!

EARTHBOUND—Rebecca Flanders
THIS TIME FOREVER—Margaret Chittenden
MOONSPELL—Regan Forest
PRINCE OF DREAMS—Carly Bishop